Awareness—and that tangible spark of attraction Cara had felt when his fingers brushed hers on the bowl—sizzled in the air between them.

She swallowed, her throat suddenly dry. But she couldn't seem to control the brutal pulse of awareness. Logan's eyes darkened as his gaze dropped to her mouth. She licked her lips, feeling his perusal like a physical caress.

What was Logan thinking? Surely he must be able to feel it, too? Whatever *it* was... Because she'd never felt like this before... Certainly never had to struggle to control her response to a man.

And if it was desire, what on earth were they supposed to do about it?

She jumped up, suddenly desperate to break the tension... But as she went to lift his empty bowl, he snagged her wrist.

Sensation pulsed and flared, the hot rock between her thighs becoming molten as their gazes locked again.

"Stay out of my way," he murmured, the hard line of his jaw and the dark arousal in his eyes making it clear he was holding on to his control with an effort.

Hot Winter Escapes

Sun, snow and sexy seductions...

Whether it's a trip to the Swiss Alps or a rendezvous on a gorgeous Hawaiian beach, warming up in front of the fire or basking in the sizzling sun, these billion-dollar getaways provide the perfect backdrops for even more scorching winter romances and passionately-ever-afters!

Escape to some winter sun in...

Bound by Her Baby Revelation by Cathy Williams

An Heir Made in Hawaii by Emmy Grayson

Claimed by the Crown Prince by Abby Green

One Forbidden Night in Paradise by Louise Fuller

And get cozy in these luxurious snowy hideaways...

A Nine-Month Deal with Her Husband
by Joss Wood

Snowbound with the Irresistible Sicilian
by Maya Blake

Undoing His Innocent Enemy
by Heidi Rice

In Bed with Her Billionaire Bodyguard
by Pippa Roscoe

All available now!

Heidi Rice

UNDOING HIS INNOCENT ENEMY

HARLEQUIN®
PRESENTS™

Recycling programs for this product may not exist in your area.

ISBN-13: 978-1-335-59316-0

Undoing His Innocent Enemy

Copyright © 2023 by Heidi Rice

For questions and comments about the quality of this book, please contact us at CustomerService@Harlequin.com.

Harlequin Enterprises ULC
22 Adelaide St. West, 41st Floor
Toronto, Ontario M5H 4E3, Canada
www.Harlequin.com

Printed in U.S.A.

USA TODAY bestselling author **Heidi Rice** lives in London, England. She is married with two teenage sons—which gives her rather too much of an insight into the male psyche—and also works as a film journalist. She adores her job, which involves getting swept up in a world of high emotions; sensual excitement; funny, feisty women; sexy, tortured men; and glamorous locations where laundry doesn't exist. Once she turns off her computer, she often does chores—usually involving laundry!

Books by Heidi Rice

Harlequin Presents

Banished Prince to Desert Boss
Revealing Her Best Kept Secret
Stolen for His Desert Throne
Redeemed by My Forbidden Housekeeper

Billion-Dollar Christmas Confessions

Unwrapping His New York Innocent

Passionately Ever After...

A Baby to Tame the Wolfe

Visit the Author Profile page
at Harlequin.com for more titles.

To Rob and our beautiful boys, Joey and Luca, who shared a marvelous adventure to Finnish Lapland with me once upon a time. So glad I finally managed to feature that wild winter landscape in a book!

CHAPTER ONE

CARA DOYLE EXHALED SLOWLY, allowing her breath to plume in the icy air. She lifted the camera she'd spent a small fortune on and watched the lynx in the view-finder as it prowled across the powdery snow.

She had been trailing the female huntress for over a week—in between shifts as a barista at a resort hotel in Saariselkä—but today she'd got so many exceptional shots excitement made her heart rate soar. Which was good because, with the temperature plummeting to minus thirty degrees this morning, she couldn't spend much longer out here before she froze.

A shiver ran through her body as the camera's shutter purred through its twenty frames per second. Even with six layers of thermal clothing she could feel the cold embalming her. She ignored the discomfort. This moment was the culmination of six months' work doing crummy jobs in a succession of Lapland hotels and resorts, all through the summer and autumn, to pay for her trip studying the behaviour of the famously elusive wildcats for her breakout portfolio as a wild-life photographer.

The lynx's head lifted, her silvery gaze locking on Cara's.

Hello, there, girl, you're grand, aren't you? Just a few more shots, I promise. Then I'll be leaving you in peace.

Cara's heart rose into her throat. The picture in her viewfinder was so stunning she could hardly breathe—the lynx's graceful feline form stood stock-still, almost as if posing for the shot. Her tawny white fur blended into the glittering landscape before she ducked beneath the snow-laden branches of the frozen spruce trees and disappeared into the monochromatic beauty of the boreal forest.

Cara waited a few more minutes. But the lynx was gone.

She rolled onto her back, stared up at the pearly sky through the trees. It was almost three o'clock—darkness would be falling soon, with only four hours of daylight at this time of year in Finnish Lapland. She had to get back to the skimobile she'd left on the edge of the forest so she didn't disturb the wildcat's habitat.

But she took a few precious moments, her lips lifting beneath the layers protecting her face from the freezing air.

It only took a few heartbeats though to realise her body temperature was dropping from lack of movement. It would be no good getting the shots she'd been working on for six months through summer, autumn and finally into the short crisp winter days, if she froze to death before she could sell them.

She levered herself onto her feet and began the trek

back to the snowmobile, picking up her pace as twilight edged in around her.

Feck, exactly how long had she been out here?

It had only seemed like minutes but, when she was totally focussed on her work, time tended to dissolve as she hunted for that single perfect shot.

At last, she saw the small skimobile where she'd left it, parked near the hide she'd been using for weeks.

She packed the camera away in its insulated box in the saddlebag, aware that her hands were getting clumsy, the piercing cold turning to a numb pain.

Not good.

The delight and excitement at finally capturing the creature she'd been trailing for months began to turn to dismay though as she switched on the ignition, and nothing happened. Annoyed, she went for option two. Grabbing the start cord, she tugged hard. Again, nothing, not even the clunking sound of the engine turning over.

Don't panic...you're grand...you know the protocol.

But even as she tried to calm herself and continued yanking the cord, all the reasons why she shouldn't have followed the lynx so far into the national forest, why she shouldn't have stayed out so long, bombarded her tired mind.

Eventually, she was forced to give up on starting the snowmobile. Her arms hurt and she was losing what was left of her strength, plus sweating under the layers of clothing only made her colder. Maybe the engine had frozen—it had been inactive here too long. She should have left it running, but she hadn't expected to stay out so long and fuel cost a fortune. She fished the satellite phone out of her pack.

There was no phone signal this far north, and no communities nearby. She knew there were rumours of some reclusive US-Finnish billionaire, who lived in the uninhabited frozen wilderness on the far side of the national forest in a stunning glass house few people had ever seen or located... The resort workers whispered about him because apparently there was some tragic story involving the murder of his parents, and the fortune he had inherited as a kid before he disappeared from the public eye. But whatever the details were, they hadn't reached Ireland, and she couldn't rely on stumbling across some mythical Fortress of Solitude in the middle of nowhere—which could be hundreds of miles away. If it even existed at all.

She tuned into the last signal she'd used.

'Mayday, Mayday. I'm in the n-national forest about f-forty miles north-east of Saariselkä. My vehicle won't start. Please respond.'

Her eyelids drooped, the strange numbness wrapping around her ribs and slowing her breathing, as the last of the sunlight disappeared. She continued to broadcast as her energy drained.

If she could just sleep for a minute, she'd be fine.

No, don't sleep, Cara.

Just when it seemed the situation couldn't possibly get any worse, she felt the first swirl of wind, the prickle of ice on her face.

What the...?

There had been no suggestion of a snowstorm

today in the weather forecast or on the radar. Because she'd checked.

But as the swirl lifted and twisted, and a whistling howl picked up through the canyon of trees, turning the winter silence into a wall of terrifying sound, she could barely hear her own voice, still shouting out the Mayday.

She burrowed into the gathering drift beside the broken snowmobile, to shelter from the wind. No one had responded. No one was coming. The battery light on the phone started to wink, the only thing she could see in the white-out.

Her mother's voice, practical, and tired, hissed through her consciousness. Bringing back their last frustrating conversation two days ago.

'You're a fine one...why would you want to go all the way there when we have more than enough creatures here to photograph on the farm?'

'Because a wildlife photographer photographs creatures in the wild, Mammy, not cows and sheep.'

'Shouldn't you be settling already? You're twenty-one and have barely had a boyfriend. All your brothers are having babies already.'

Because my brothers have no desire to get out of County Wexford, just like you, Mammy.

The answer she'd wanted to say swirled in her head, the icy cold making her eyes water.

Don't you dare cry, Cara Doyle, or your eyelids will stick to your eyeballs and then where will you be?

Everywhere was starting to hurt now. The six layers of expensive thermal clothing she'd maxed out one of her many credit cards to buy felt like a layer of tissue paper against the frigid wind.

The dying phone, forgotten in her hand, crackled and then barked.

'Yes… Yes?' she croaked out on a barely audible sob.

Please let that be someone coming to rescue me.

'The cat's lights. Turn them on.' The furious voice seemed to shoot through the wind and burrow into her brain.

Relief swept through her. She nodded, her throat too raw to reply. She pushed herself into the wind with the last of her strength. Her bones felt so brittle now she was sure they were frozen too. She flicked the switch, then collapsed over the seat.

The single yellow beam shone out into the storm—and made her think of all those stories she'd heard as a child, in Bible study as she prepped for her first holy communion, about the white light of Jesus beckoning you, which you saw before death.

Sister Mary Clodagh had always scared the hell out of them with that tale.

But Cara didn't feel scared now, she just felt exhausted.

Her sore eyelids drooped.

'Keep talking.' The gruff voice on the phone reverberated in her skull.

She pressed the mouthpiece to her lips, mumbled what she could through the layers of her balaclavas.

'Louder,' the shout barked back.

'I'm trying…' she managed. Her fingers and face

didn't hurt any more, because the embalming warmth pressed against her chest like a hot blanket.

Whoever Mr Angry is, he'd better be getting a move on.

A dark shape appeared in the pearly beam, the outline making her think of the majestic brown bears she'd spent the summer in Lapland observing and photographing… The hum of an engine cut through the howling wind as the bear got closer. It detached from its base, the dark shape looming over her.

Piercing silvery blue eyes locked on hers through the thin strip of skin visible under his helmet and above his face coverings and reminded her of the lynx—who she'd photographed what felt like several lifetimes ago.

Hard hands clasped her arms, lifting her. She tried to struggle free, scared her bones would snap.

'Don't fight me,' the bear shouted. 'Stay awake, don't sleep.'

Why was the bear shaking her? Was he attacking her? Shouldn't he be hibernating?

She tried to reply, but the words got stuck in her throat as his big body shielded her from the ice storm. The slaps were firm, but not painful, glancing off her cheek.

'Your name, tell me your name. Don't sleep.'

Why did a bear want to know her name? And how come it could talk?

She couldn't say anything, it hurt to speak. It hurt to even think.

She just wanted to sleep.

She heard cursing, angry, upset, reminding her of her father when he came home from the pub... So long ago now. Good riddance.

Don't sleep or he will come back and call you names again...

But as she found herself bundled onto a raft and being whisked through the storm, the icy wind shifting into a magical dance of blue and green light, the twinkle of stars like fairy lights in the canopy of darkness over her head, a comforting rumble seeped into her soul and chased away the old fear of her da.

Then the brutal, beautiful exhaustion claimed her at last.

Logan Arto Coltan III rode the utility snowmobile into the underground garage of his home and slammed the heavy machine into park.

He swore viciously as he jumped from the saddle and raced to the flatbed he'd hooked up to load supplies.

'Wake up,' he shouted at the body lying on top of the boxes of canned goods and frozen meat he'd been transporting when he'd picked up the Mayday. Accidentally.

He never monitored the emergency frequencies, but the dial must have slipped after he had called his supply pilot.

Why had he answered the call? He should have ignored it. Why hadn't he?

The person's eyelids—the long lashes white with

frost—fluttered open. Revealing bright young eyes, coloured a deep emerald green.

He felt the odd jolt of something… And ignored it. Not unconscious. Yet.

'Stay with me,' he said, then repeated it in Finnish—just in case English wasn't their first language—as he assessed the person's size under their bulky outdoor wear. Around five six. Probably a woman, he decided, as he stripped off the outer layers of his own clothing. The garage was kept at nineteen degrees, so he didn't overheat before removing his snowsuit to enter the house. But right now, he needed to be able to move, so he could get this fool inside.

Once he'd got down to his undershirt and trackpants, he headed to the garage's small utility room and grabbed the first-aid box. Dragging off his last pair of gloves, he found the thermometer, shoved it into his pants' pocket and returned to the trailer.

If this idiot had managed to give themselves hypothermia, he'd have to call an air ambulance.

He frowned, struggling to focus around the anger—and panic—that had been roiling in his gut ever since he'd answered the call.

Lifting the woman, he placed her as gently as he could over his shoulder. If she was hypothermic sudden movements could trigger a fatal heart arrhythmia. He toted her across the concrete space to climb the steps into the house. His home, ever since his grandfather had died ten years ago. A space no one else had ever entered while he was in residence.

'Avata,' he shouted to the house's integrated smart

system, ignoring the roll and pitch in his gut as the locks clicked and he kicked the heavy metal door open with his boot.

'*Tuli päälle,*' he added to instruct the fire to come on, as he walked into the vast living area. He set the girl on one of the sunken sofas that surrounded a stone fire pit.

The orange flames leapt up and reflected off the panoramic window that opened the luxury space into the winter landscape beyond, obscuring the night-time view of the forest gorge lit by the eerie glow of moon-light.

Safe.

He'd always been safe here, alone. But as he peeled off the woman's layers of headwear, a tumble of wavy reddish-blonde hair was revealed and the strange jolt returned, making him not feel safe any more.

Focus, Logan. You had no choice. It was bring her here or let her die.

She was still staring at him, her eyes glazed but somehow alert, in a way that immediately made him suspicious.

What the hell had she been doing on his land? So far from the nearest centre of civilisation, alone, as night fell?

'How do you feel?' he asked as he reached into his back pocket to grab the thermometer.

'C-c-cold,' she said, starting to shiver violently.

He nodded. Shivering was good.

He shook the thermometer, snapping off its protective covering. Then he pressed his thumb to her chapped bottom lip and placed it under her tongue.

He clicked the timer on his watch, to count down four minutes.

'Wh-wh…?'

'Don't talk.' He glared at the girl, who was staring at him now with a dazed, confused expression in those bright eyes as she continued to shudder.

Not so good.

The timer dinged.

He tugged out the thermometer. Ninety-four point nine degrees.

He cursed softly.

Anything below ninety-five was mild hypothermia. *Great*.

'Come on.' He dumped the thermometer on the coffee table, stood, and scooped her carefully into his arms. 'We must get you warm,' he said as he strode towards the wooden staircase that led to the guest bedroom that had never been used on the ground level.

As he marched through the house, with her still shivering, he considered his options.

Perhaps he should call the EMT station in Saariselkä. But she was young, still lucid, looked healthy enough. And he'd located her fairly quickly. Plus she was conscious and her temperature was on the cusp. If he could get it back past ninety-five quickly, there would be no need for hospital treatment and hopefully no ill effects. It would take over an hour for the EMTs to get here even in a chopper and the storm still stood between them.

And he'd be damned if he'd give up the location of

his home to help out a stranger before he absolutely had to… And before he knew who this person was, and what she had been doing on his land—getting herself lost in a snowstorm.

That said, he thought grimly as he began stripping off the wet outer layers of her clothing, while she stood shivering and docile… This promised to be a very long night.

CHAPTER TWO

WHERE AM I? Who is this guy? And why don't I care that he's taking off my clothing?

Another violent shudder racked Cara's body as her rescuer kneeled in front of her and lifted each foot to tug off her snow boots. She had to grasp his shoulder to stop herself from falling on top of him—but he seemed oblivious, his movements swift and deliberate as he peeled off her sodden snowsuit and the ski-pants beneath.

His shoulder flexed beneath her ungloved fingers making her aware of the thin thermal undershirt he'd stripped down to—which moulded to his impressive physique like a second skin. Another series of shudders turned her body into a human castanet.

Maybe I don't care because I'm exhausted. And I'd rather be here, wherever here is, than out in the storm.

Something about Mr Angry felt, if not safe, exactly, because he was big and grumpy, then at least not dangerous.

'Wh-who a-a-are y-you?' she managed through the

shudders, so exhausted now she was astonished she was still upright.

'Save your energy,' he said, not answering her question. 'You will need it.'

He stood, and his piercing silvery blue gaze locked on her face, the icy glare trapping her like a tractor beam. Suspicion flashed across his features. His jaw hardened under a rough stubble, which looked as if he'd forgotten to shave for a while, rather than grown it intentionally. His hair was a thick dark brown and long enough to touch his collar. He swept the unkempt waves off his forehead, but they dropped back again almost immediately. He didn't look as if he'd had a proper haircut in years, Cara thought vaguely. How odd, that he couldn't afford a haircut, when his place—if this place was his—looked so exclusive.

Much like the living area they had first entered, the sparsely furnished bedroom had a massive glass wall at the far end of the room, which took in the view of snow-laden forest and wide open sky, the darkness sprinkled with stars and brightened by the blue glow of a full moon…

His home was beyond stunning, a steel and glass minimalist palace that wouldn't look out of place in a glossy travel magazine. Or a Superman comic.

A Fortress of Solitude… She tried to focus her mind, grasp hold of that thought and the strange feeling of *déjà vu*. Why did she feel as if she knew this place? Or knew of it?

He was still staring at her as he pulled the zip down on her fleece and tugged her arms out. The fierce expression didn't just look suspicious now, it looked annoyed, and he was making no effort to hide it.

But as he knelt in front of her again, to take off her sweatpants, his hair flopped over his forehead again. She yearned to sweep the unruly waves away from his face, so she could see more of him, because however annoyed he was, he also fascinated her. Those pale, piercing eyes and the sharp angles of his face were not softened at all by his rugged, unkempt appearance. Although she'd only ever had the urge to photograph wildlife before now, she would love to photograph him, because there was something about him that seemed untamed despite the sophistication of his home.

She resisted the urge to touch him though, because her fingers were still cramping and she barely had the strength to stand—let alone lift her arm. Plus, she got the definite impression from his taciturn behaviour, he would not welcome her touch.

He remained silent as he continued to strip her out of the heavy clothing with brutal efficiency until all she wore were her panties, her bra, her thick woolly socks and the skintight thermal tights, which left very little to anyone's imagination.

She used all her strength to fold one arm across her breasts, feeling hideously exposed all of a sudden. And vulnerable. But her whole body was so shattered it was hard to muster a blush—even though, being Irish and a redhead, blushing was one of her superpowers.

What was worse than feeling naked in front of him, though, was feeling like a burden. She hated to be a burden—had always been self-sufficient, ever since her father had left and her mother had spent her evenings crying herself to sleep when she'd thought Cara and her brothers couldn't hear her…

Why are you thinking about your deadbeat da again?

The thought echoed through her foggy brain.

Luckily, she was too tired to muster the energy to be embarrassed about her dependence on Mr Grumpy as he leant past her to strip back the heavy duvet and then scooped her up and laid her in the middle of the enormous bed.

He tucked the quilt under her chin as she continued to shudder and shake. She still couldn't feel her feet, but her fingers and face were starting to burn as the blood flow returned.

The sheets smelled of laundry soap and a tantalising combination of bergamot and pine.

'I'm going to get a heated blanket and something hot to drink,' he said, his gruff accent a strange transatlantic mix of American and Scandinavian. 'We need to raise your temperature. Don't sleep or I'll have to wake you.'

She managed a nod, before watching him stride from the room.

As he disappeared through the doorway, she forced her gaze back towards the magnificent view through the room's glass wall.

The shaking had downgraded to a shiver when he finally returned. Somehow, she'd managed to keep her eyes open, even though the rest of her had melted into the mattress.

He perched on the edge of the bed, then tugged the duvet down to place the heated blanket next to her skin. He broke a heat pack over his knee and placed it under her neck. She flinched as he bundled her up in the blanket and quilt.

'I-it h-hurts,' she said, blinking furiously to hold back the tears scorching her eyes.

She'd rather die than cry in front of this guy.

'I know,' he said, but didn't offer any words of comfort or reassurance.

Your bedside manner really sucks, fella.

The antagonistic thought galvanised her despite her misery, at least a little bit, as he lifted her into a sitting position, banded his arm around her back and then reached for the hot mug he'd brought in with the blanket and heat pack.

As she inhaled, the scent of him got trapped in her lungs, and she realised the tantalising aroma of bergamot and pine belonged to him.

Why did recognising his scent feel stupidly intimate? And make her feel even more compromised and vulnerable?

'Drink,' he ordered as he pressed the mug to her lips.

She gulped and spluttered, her tongue numb and her lips chapped. He ignored her grunts of protest, which somehow made her feel less compromised, keeping the mug pressed to her sore lips until she had consumed nearly half of the hot sweet mint tea.

At last, he let her lie down and took her temperature again.

As he checked it, the sharp frown on his face levelled out, a fraction.

'Ninety-five.' He stood, making her even more aware of his height.

He was so tall, his rangy body intimidatingly muscular. Whatever he did for a living, he was not idle.

All the better to rescue you with, Cara. Be grateful.

'Looks like you'll live,' he added, with a lack of enthusiasm that might have stung if she had been able to muster anything other than the deep desire to sleep for several millennia.

Trust me to get rescued by the most reluctant knight ever.

'I'll check on you during the night,' he added. 'Sleep now.'

Her eyelids shut on his command, but as she was whisked away by the foggy exhaustion—her body finally having stopped shivering long enough to sink into the mattress the rest of the way—all she could think was how odd it was that even though she was pretty sure she didn't like him, and he *really* didn't like her, she was glad he would be near tonight.

When she woke the next morning, Cara had a vague recollection of being awakened during the night by her rescuer. He'd taken her temperature and adjusted the heated blanket a few times… As she flexed tired, aching limbs in the huge bed, and inhaled that tantalising scent again, she realised the electric blanket was gone. So he must have retrieved it, to allow her to sleep comfortably during the night.

She blinked down tears as she turned towards the enormous picture window.

Now, don't you dare go getting emotional for no reason, Cara Doyle. He only did what any decent person would do in the circumstances. He could hardly be leaving you out there to freeze.

But even though she knew the emotion was simply relief after the painful, frankly terrifying ordeal of being stranded in the snowstorm, not sure if she would survive it, and that odd feeling of intimacy as he'd tended her through the night, it was hard not to feel indebted. And pathetically grateful.

For a guy who clearly did not want her in his home, he'd been remarkably diligent. And though brusque, also gentle with her.

Unlike the night before, when there had been a clear view of the forest through the glass wall, snow swirled now, and ice drifted across the landscape. The snow-laden forest on the edge of the tundra was obscured by what looked like another approaching storm.

She forced herself out of the bed, glad to discover her legs were still in working order, even if she did feel winded by the time she had crossed the room.

She pressed her nose to the frosted glass. Even though she was in only her thermal tights and her underwear, the ambient temperature in the room felt warm and comfortable. Mr Grumpy's Fortress had much better insulation than her mammy's farm in

Wexford, that was for sure, where she and her brothers had worn their outside coats indoors when the temperature had dipped to ten degrees. They'd have frozen solid in minus thirty.

There you go, thinking of home again.

She admonished herself. She had never been sentimental about Ireland, not since she'd left to pursue her dream of becoming a wildlife photographer, after spending years as a child watching and observing and finally learning to document the birds and small creatures in and around the farm.

The photos.

Panic pierced her heart.

She'd left her camera with the shots she'd taken of the lynx in the saddlebags of her broken snowmobile. The shots she'd nearly died to acquire… And which even now might be buried under a snowdrift.

She needed to thank Mr Grumpy for his help and get back to her snowmobile. But already she suspected the snowstorm was going to make that hard. And her weakened condition probably wasn't going to help either.

She wiped the mist off the glass as she spotted something… A large snowmobile driving across the frozen lake. The figure bundled in the necessary six or seven layers of winter clothing in the saddle handled the lumbering machine with casual grace, making him instantly recognisable.

Mr Grumpy. Aka the guy who had rescued her and tended her throughout the night, but whose name she didn't know.

A strange shudder shot through her, bringing with it a spurt of adrenaline to jolt her out of her maudlin thoughts of her family's farm—and her panic about the precious cargo she'd left in the forest. She tracked the snowmobile as it drove towards the house then disappeared beneath her, into what had to be the garage where she could remember them arriving the night before.

Before he'd carried her first into the vast living area then into this bedroom.

A weight formed in her throat, then swooped down into her belly as she recalled the feel of his hands, impersonal but also gentle, as he'd stripped her wet clothing off. The feel of his shoulder tensing under her hand, his arm braced against her back as he forced the hot drink on her, and those piercing silvery blue eyes locked on her face, studying her…

Sensation rippled over her skin, a lot more vivid now than it had been last night, when her brain had been foggy and her body too tired to experience much of anything but the intense cold, and those violent shudders.

Stop thinking about him. And figure out how to rescue your camera.

She pressed her forehead to the glass. And evened her breathing, trying to ignore the unfamiliar sensations rippling over her skin. She needed to formulate a plan as soon as she could, because the lynx photos were the crowning glory that would help her sell her Lapland portfolio to the stock photo site she'd been schmoozing for months.

She needed that income to pay off the credit cards she'd maxed out in the last six months to set up in Lapland. To take the next step in her career plan, she had to free up more time to observe and study the behaviour of the wildlife she wished to document and less time in the menial jobs—barista, waitress, hotel cleaner—that had just about kept her solvent…

Which would mean begging Mr Grumpy to take her to her machine, and—if it couldn't be fixed—then back to Saariselkä.

The good news was, he was clearly more than happy to travel in a storm. And, wherever he'd been just now, he was back. Not so good was the fact that—after she'd hunted the room—the rest of her clothes seemed to have disappeared, and she was now totally breathless.

Also not good… From her interaction with him so far, she did not think her host was going to be too pleased about being asked to do her another enormous favour.

Plus, charm had never been one of Cara's strengths. She knew that. She'd always been outspoken and fiercely independent, especially with men—thanks, Da—which was probably why she'd never had much luck in the boyfriend department. Something her mother had pointed out on numerous occasions.

But you're not trying to seduce him, Cara, you're just going to ask him for a favour. So it's all good.

After taking a hot shower in the adjoining bathroom—another striking, intimidatingly masculine and scrupulously clean architectural marvel made in quartz and glass and hand-carved stone—she found an oversized sweatshirt in the chest of drawers. On her it made a passable mini dress. At least it covered her backside, so she felt less naked once she'd put her tights back on. Finally, she felt human again.

But as she ventured out of the bedroom in search of her host, she could feel the hot brick dropping further into her stomach and jiggling about like a jumping bean. Which was just plain peculiar.

She didn't get nervous around men. It was surely just that she owed this guy more than she'd ever owed any man. And now she must ask for more.

But then, she'd never see him again after today. And she had a feeling he would be more than happy to see the back of her. So there was that.

Logan dumped the coffee jug back on the plate, sloshing the fresh brew over the kitchen counter. He gulped down a mouthful of hot black liquid and swallowed, focussing on the burn in his throat.

He was so damn mad his hands were shaking. He clasped the mug tight and willed them to stop, not caring that the hot china scalded his palms.

He'd found the camera in her gear on the disabled snowmobile—and left it there. Just as he'd figured, the girl's appearance on the edge of his land hadn't been a coincidence. The hypothermia and the snowmobile's engine failure had been real. But she had risked her life to get a shot of him and his home—that had to be the explanation.

His grandfather had warned him long ago, the

press was his enemy—that it was the media who had put a target on his parents' backs twenty years ago, reporting on their volatile marriage—the endless cycle of public arguments, private feuds, bitter silences, attention-seeking reconciliations—in minute and exploitative detail.

Logan thrust his fingers through his hair, the memory of the camera flashes like lightning bolts, the shouted demands for him to look up, to tell them how he felt about his parents' deaths hitting him like body blows all over again. He shuddered, remembering the sight of the muddy earth of their graves on that cold November morning. Panic assailed him, as another more visceral memory pressed at his consciousness.

He shoved it back.

He hadn't been able to cry at their funeral—had struggled to feel anything at all—cast into a media storm that had terrified him.

He'd been ten years old. An orphan. Trapped alone on the Coltan estate in Rhode Island with a staff of people paid to care for him. His life had been ruled and administered by a board of trustees until the Finnish grandfather he'd never met had brought him here.

And saved him. Protected him from all the people, so many people, who had wanted to exploit his loss.

He stared at the furious storm building outside the glass. And his hands stopped shaking at last.

His sanctuary. A place disconnected from the outside world. A place he'd built himself—in secret—at nineteen, because he couldn't bear to stay in his grandfather's A-frame house any more, without the old man there.

And now she had invaded it.

Hell, she hadn't just invaded it, she'd tricked him into bringing her here.

Into exposing himself all over again to the questions he couldn't answer as the memories tore at his chest.

'Hiya.'

He swung round to see the cause of his fury standing in his kitchen. She wore one of his sweatshirts, which didn't do much to cover the long, toned legs he'd noticed last night. The strange sensation in his gut flared, right alongside his anger.

He stared at her. Having someone—*anyone*—sharing his space felt wrong. An intrusion that he had never allowed, but there was something about having her standing on the other side of the kitchen counter, after the night he'd spent tending her, that felt wrong and yet also… Not.

'You don't need people, Arto. Nature is better. It does not scheme and exploit. It just is. Your mother was weak—she sought the limelight and was punished for it. You are not weak. You don't need those things.'

He ruthlessly ignored the flicker of exhilaration in his gut as his grandfather's voice echoed in his head.

Johannes Makinen had not been a talkative man. Never tactile or nurturing. But as austere as he had always been, he had also been as steady as the seasons, and fiercely protective of the broken boy Logan had been when he had first arrived in his mother's homeland, crippled by a fear of people that had taken years to become manageable.

The solitude, the silence here, had helped him survive those early years when he had been scared of every sound, every voice, except his grandfather's. He could not bear to be touched for so long, he had learned to survive without that too. And eventually the nightmares that tore him from sleep and dragged him back into the middle of that terrible night had died.

And that was when he'd understood, his grandfather was right. Even as his physical needs had changed as a teenager and eventually a man, he had learned to deny them—because he never wanted to be that broken again.

Something this woman would never understand.

But even as he tried to convince himself he did not want her here, he found himself studying her lithe physique and the flicker became a warm weight in his abdomen.

She cleared her throat, her pale skin bright with colour.

'I'd be after thanking you for last night,' she said. Her accent had a musical lilt that didn't match the sharp edges of Scandinavia, or the casual sway of the US. 'You... Well, you saved my life.'

The flush fired across her collarbone and made him notice the fascinating sprinkle of freckles there—and the rise and fall of her breasts under the baggy sweatshirt.

He gave a stiff nod. He didn't want her gratitude. He wanted her gone.

'You… You never told me your name,' she asked, as if she didn't know.

She was a good actress, he'd give her that, the curious light in her gaze almost credible. But he only became more annoyed when he noticed that the vivid green of her irises matched the deep striking emerald of the aurora borealis.

'Logan Colton,' he said, knowing he was not giving anything away that she didn't already know.

'Logan…? Colt…?'

Her eyebrows launched up her forehead, then her head whipped around, taking in the beamed ceiling, the huge open-plan space where he lived and which he had built on the footprint of his grandfather's old home.

'You're the billionaire recluse… This is it. The Fortress of Solitude… Of course,' she whispered, her voice low with either awe or astonishment, it was hard to tell. But then it hardly mattered, because this was no doubt an act for his benefit. 'You're the guy they talk about. You actually *exist*?' She gaped at him, and he realised she was worthy of an award—either that or she was not as smart as the fierce intelligence in her eyes suggested. 'I thought for sure that was a myth. Or a fairy tale.'

A fairy tale? Seriously?

He bristled. He didn't know any fairy tales. But what he did know was they were fanciful nonsense designed to scare young children. And he had never been a child. Or scared of imaginary things. Because he knew exactly what terrors real life could hold.

Rain, endless rain, pounding down onto the dirty pavement. The scent of blood filling his nostrils, the cold dead weight pushing him into the filthy ground. His mother's broken screams. The pop of bullets like party balloons bursting. The fear clawing at his throat, making his heart rate accelerate to bursting…

He closed his eyes briefly to shove away the visions pushing into his consciousness again for the first time in years…

'Monsters exist, Arto. And they all take human form.'

His grandfather's voice eased the pain in his chest and pushed the worst of the memories back into the darkness, where they belonged.

'I'm sure I would have figured it out a lot sooner if I hadn't been so exhausted last night.' Her musical accent drew him sharply back to the present.

She wrapped her arms around her waist and gave a small shudder as if the memory of her ordeal disturbed her.

'Do you really live here all alone, then?' she asked, changing the subject. But then her eyes widened. 'I'm sorry, I'm sure that's not my business at all. I talk too much.'

Two things they could agree on.

'You're not a big talker, are you?' she added. 'Even for a Finnish person.'

Apparently, she was more observant than she appeared. But again, that was not a surprise—given that she was probably a journalist.

Her stomach made a loud growling sound, reminding him she hadn't eaten yet today.

He let his gaze drift down her frame, annoyed when it lingered on the soft swell of her breasts beneath his old sweatshirt again.

He forced his gaze back to her flushed face, angry he had let himself get sucked into that response again. He didn't need human contact, and that must include women. He had convinced himself long ago his hand would do if he needed relief.

But having her in his home was distracting. And aggravating, for more than one reason. Already she was testing the boundaries he had made himself live by. And he hated that even more than the predatory reason for her intrusion into his home.

'There is food, help yourself,' he said, suddenly desperate to be somewhere she was not. His response to her would surely fade if he was not near her.

But as he walked past her, heading back towards his workshop, she reached out and touched his bare arm.

He was so shocked by the unsolicited contact, he flinched.

She dropped her hand instantly, but the ripple of sensation still buzzed across his senses in a way that only disturbed him more.

'I'm sorry…' she murmured.

He stiffened, hating the look in her gaze—confused, surprised but also somehow full of empathy.

'Where are you going?' she asked.

'Work,' he said.

'But… I wanted to ask you…' She swallowed, looking unsure of herself, again. 'Could you give me a lift back to my snowmobile today? So I can get out of your hair.'

'No.' He couldn't be around her, let her touch him again, until he was fully prepared for that contact, and his confusing response to it.

'Why not?' Her guileless expression only infuriated him more.

The truth—that her touch had had a profound effect on him—would make him look weak and foolish. So, he seized on all the other reasons why he could not take her anywhere today.

'The storm will become impassable,' he said, which was only the truth.

She did not know he had found her camera. If she lied about it, he would know the truth. So he added, 'And before you leave, you must tell me why you are really here.'

Her mouth went slack, those deep emerald eyes widening even further. 'But... You know why. My skimobile broke down in the snowstorm and you rescued me.'

'That is not the truth,' he said, or certainly not the whole truth. And until she told him that, he knew he could not trust her.

She simply blinked, as if struggling to process his statement. Another act.

He walked past her, the silence behind him layered with shock.

Despite his anger, and the disturbing unease—that visceral awareness that had made his skin prickle and the warm weight in his gut start to pulse—he felt a little of his power returning as he left the room.

At least he had finally found a way to shut her up.

CHAPTER THREE

CARA STARED AFTER Logan Colton's retreating back—
and his ridiculously broad shoulders—as her jaw
dropped so fast she was surprised it didn't bounce
off the quartz floor tiles.

She was completely and utterly speechless as he
disappeared through the large doorway that led who
knew where in this enormous house.

What just happened?

She ran the conversation they'd had back through
her head.

Not that you could really call it a conversation—
given that the man had uttered all of about ten words
on his end of it.

She'd thanked him and asked him politely to return
her to her snowmobile. And okay, maybe her reaction hadn't been the best when she'd figured out who
he really was—the billionaire recluse she had been
convinced was a figment of everyone's imagination.
But hey, she'd only just recovered from a near-death
experience. And surely she could be forgiven for a
little overfamiliarity—after all, he'd seen her all but

naked the night before. And saved her from said near-death experience.

He'd looked at her with such intensity, she'd felt his gaze roam over her skin like a caress, her unbidden reaction as shocking as it was…well, shocking. For a moment she'd thought there was something there, something she probably shouldn't entertain—given her circumstances as a woman alone, in a stranger's home. But that searing gaze, dark with awareness, hadn't disgusted or unnerved her. It had made every one of her reliably dormant pheromones rejoice as if they were spending St Pat's Day getting plastered in Dublin's Temple Bar—instead of stranded in a stranger's ice palace in the middle of nowhere.

But then she'd felt him flinch at her touch, and seen the flash of fury in his eyes.

And her pheromones had stopped partying—because that look had transported her back to her family's kitchen, on the receiving end of one of her father's drunken tirades. And left her feeling miserable, and suffocated, and unfairly judged.

She was so shocked by his accusations, though, she was completely speechless for one whole minute.

But then the sense of injustice, of righteous indignation—which had got her through so much of her childhood, and finally dynamited her out of Ireland and away from the cruel memories of her father's abuse—kicked into gear.

Adrenaline charged through her veins, flushing away the last of the breathlessness that had dogged her ever since she'd woken up.

Maybe she owed Mr Grumpy her life and maybe she had invaded his privacy—something it was clear he was not happy about—and yeah, maybe she talked way too much. But what gave him the right to question her integrity? To suggest she had engineered a near-death experience… To do *what* exactly?

She shot through the doorway after him, finally finding her voice.

'Mr Colton, wait?' she shouted. The doorway led into another stunning architectural space. A wall of glass bricks revealed a panoramic view of the undulating forest rising across a gorge at the back of the property, which was blanketed in a thick layer of snow. The snow continued to cascade from the darkening sky in swirling gusts of white.

She slipped and slid in her socks on the stone floor, past the sunken fire pit and the couch she vaguely remembered being deposited on the night before. Two staircases led to other levels, one up, one down.

'Mr Colton, where are you?' she shouted, choosing the staircase down, because the staircase up might lead her to his bedroom, and she suspected heading there would not improve this situation at all.

She got no reply. Her indignation rose as she found herself lost in a complex series of passageways, lit by skylights. She walked past the door to a fully equipped gym—which had to explain those impressive pecs.

So not the point, Cara.

She didn't care if he'd saved her life. That didn't mean he got to be a judgemental jerk.

At last, she came to another staircase leading to a

covered walkway insulated against the storm outside.
It led to a large wooden structure constructed under
the trees. She spotted him through the floor-to-ceiling
glass panels on one side, standing in the light airy space,
leaning over a worktable. He had his back to her as she
burst through the door, her footsteps and heavy breathing covered by loud music—the tune one from a rock
band from decades ago—blaring from an impressive
sound system.

The workshop—for that was surely what it was—
was the only messy place in the whole house, every
available surface strewn with drawings, sketches, and
an array of tools.

Organised chaos was what it seemed.

But then she saw the sculptures that stood in the
far corner. Lifesize renderings of animal and plant
life—the most striking of which was a black bear in
full attack mode.

She drew a staggered breath…

The sculpture was exquisite. The bear looked so
lifelike, but also stylised, its lumbering body rendered
in the layered grain of the wood, the intent in its eyes,
somehow both real and yet also mythic. The carving
captured the power and strength as well as the natural grace of a species she had observed herself during
the summer months.

Even her photographs could not have captured the
magnificent creature so perfectly.

She stood spellbound for a moment.

But then her host turned, sensing her presence, and

that searing blue gaze fixed on her face. He barked something in Finnish and the music died.

All she could hear was her own breathing.

The deep frown didn't alleviate the dark intensity in his expression one bit.

Breathe, Cara.

She forced herself to suck in a breath past the hot lump that had got jammed in her throat... And now sank between her thighs.

Oh, for the love of...

'Leave,' he said, in that charmingly erudite way he had—as if every word cost him a billion euros to utter.

But before he had a chance to turn his back on her again, she managed to locate her outrage, which had momentarily malfunctioned in the face of his staggering arrogance. And the striking beauty of his work.

'That's exactly what I want to be doing. But the storm is not my fault...'

'Leave my *workshop*,' he said as if she were an eejit, while completely missing the point. 'I want you where I am not.'

She would have congratulated herself on managing to get another whole sentence out of him—which, from the rusty sound of his voice, she suspected was an achievement. Except what he had said was just as rude and dictatorial as his two-syllable answers.

'Look, fella, it's clear you want me here even less than I want to be here.' She began again, holding on to her temper with an effort. From the rigid line of his jaw and the fierce suspicion in his gaze, she suspected losing her cool would only fuel his bad opinion of her.

'But that doesn't give you the right to insult me. Or imply that I tricked my way into your home when I was about to die of exposure last night.'

He leaned back against the worktable, crossed his arms over that wide chest—pumping up those magnificent biceps, annoyingly—and glared.

'You wish to play games?' he said, making even less sense now than he had before.

'What games?' she asked. Was that a trick question? Surely it had to be. As she had no fecking clue what games he was talking about.

'I know why you are really here.'

'You… What?' Her voice trailed off, anger and frustration replaced with confusion.

'I found the camera.' He spat the last word, as if it were an obscenity.

Okay, there was clearly some misunderstanding here. Because he was looking at her as if her camera were an unexploded nuclear warhead.

If only she'd listened more carefully to her fellow barista Issi's stories about this guy, then she might have some clue what his problem was. But whatever his problem was, she needed to get to the bottom of it, before she exploded from frustration…and that damn throbbing in her gut got any more forceful—which had no business being there at all.

'You found my equipment in the snowmobile?' So that was where he had just been.

He gave a curt nod.

'Did you bring it back with you?' she asked, the

flicker of hope in her chest almost painful. Maybe her work hadn't been lost.

'No,' he said.

The hope guttered out. And she had the stupid urge to cry. Six months' work. Lost. Not to mention the thousands of pounds' worth of priceless equipment that was now probably close to being frozen solid. That camera had been her future. A future she hadn't been able to afford to insure.

I hate my life.

She swallowed heavily, to contain the pain. The last thing she needed right now was to show him a weakness, because she had a feeling it would only increase his contempt. From his rigid unyielding stance, it was clear he didn't have a compassionate or empathetic bone in his body.

Her gaze glided over his impressive physique, the ridges of his six-pack moulded under the skintight thermal shirt.

His very *hot* body. The man was a ride and no mistake.

She blinked.

Whoa, girl. Why are you getting fixated on his abs when it's his suspicious mind you need to concentrate on?

'Why not?' she managed, her voice breaking on the words. How hard would it have been for him to bring back her camera?

He didn't answer her perfectly reasonable question. He simply continued to glare at her—but she spotted the flicker of surprise cross his features before he could mask it.

It was only a small crack, but she'd take it.

'Why did you go out to find my snowmobile?' she asked. 'If you didn't intend to rescue my stuff?'

'To check if the machine was really broken.'

It was her turn to look surprised. Make that astonished. Exactly how cynical was he?

'You thought I faked being stranded?' she asked, even though she could see from the ice in his gaze he had thought exactly that.

He shrugged. 'Yes.'

'Why...? Why would I do that?' She knew she shouldn't be angry with him—she'd nearly died. But she was still too astonished by that brittle suspicion to be anything but dumbfounded. How could anyone be this cynical? This guarded?

'For the same reason you have the camera.'

That pale blue gaze glided over her figure. But despite the icy suspicion, all it did was make the throb in her abdomen heat.

Terrific.

'You've lost me again,' she said.

He crossed his ankles, drawing her attention to the muscles flexing in his thighs beneath the clinging brushed cotton of his sweatpants. She noticed for the first time, he wore thick woollen socks, which somehow softened the hard, unyielding stance.

But not much. Her gaze rose back to the rigid jawline, tensing under the thick stubble.

Why did he have to look so gorgeous, when he was clearly a paranoid eejit?

The quiet stretched out between them, only disturbed by the snowstorm outside the glass—its roar partially muffled by the triple glazing. She refused to say more, forced to bite her lip until he gave her an answer she could understand.

Obviously, he had decided she had some ulterior motive for being here... For nearly freezing to death yesterday. But he needed to tell her what it was, before she could defend herself.

'I know what your pictures are worth,' he said, being so cryptic it was starting to strain what was left of her patience. 'But you will never sell them.'

'You found my pictures of the lynx?' Was he some kind of wildlife photographer too? A rival? Although that made no sense either. Not only did he have a reputation for being extremely wealthy, but he also appeared to be an incredibly talented artist. Why would he be making a career for himself as a photographer when he could surely sell his artwork for a lot more?

It was his turn to frown. 'Stop the act,' he said.

The what-now...?

Frustration and fury blindsided her. She chewed on her lip, hard enough to taste blood, to hold the volatile reaction in check.

She would not let him goad her into losing her temper the rest of the way. Because she'd learnt at a young age, if someone insisted on judging you, on making you feel small and insignificant—the way her father had done so often, before he had disappeared from all their lives—the best thing to do was not let them see you cared about their opinion.

'Why don't you tell me what you think I'm guilty of? *Then* I can drop my act.' She ground out the words.

One dark brow rose up his forehead, the twist of his lips flattening into a thin, intractable line. But he remained maddeningly silent.

Her motto had always been never defend, never explain. Because in her experience, that only led to more judgement… But he was leaving her with no choice.

'But just for the record, I'm a wildlife photographer.' She pushed the words out, determined to believe them, even though up until two days ago her main source of income had been menial jobs. 'The pictures on that camera were of a female Arctic lynx, which I have been tracking for weeks. You would also have found shots on the memory card of a wild reindeer herd from last week. I shouldn't have come so far out—should not have waited until it was almost dark to restart the snowmobile. And I'm still beyond grateful you rescued me. But I don't have an ulterior motive or a hidden agenda for being here…' She glanced around the structure. 'Wherever *here* actually is. I didn't even know you were a real person until this morning. But whatever your secret is, it is safe with me. All I want to do is rescue the equipment I've maxed out all my credit cards to buy. And, if possible, save the pictures I took of the lynx, which almost cost me my life. And then I want to return to Saariselkä so I can sell them to the stock photography company I've been trying to impress for months. If that's okay with you.'

She finally ran out of breath, the effort it had taken not just to speak, but to overcome her golden rule and explain herself, leaving her exhausted again. Her whole body slumped, the starch of her justifiable anger seeping away to leave her drained.

Unfortunately, his expression remained carved in granite. It hadn't softened one iota.

Well, isn't that just grand?

'Whatever your secret is, it is safe with me.'

Something leapt in Logan's chest, something unprecedented and fierce. And dangerous.

She looked so earnest, so honest, so forthright—which was precisely why he would be a fool to believe her.

The moment of doubt, though, that she might actually be who she said she was, made him almost as angry as the flood of hunger.

Her pale skin had flushed a deep red, her eyes were bright with purpose, her stance both belligerent but also brave. Making her look even more stunning than she had this morning when he'd first encountered her in his kitchen.

The desire, thick and insistent, which he had not even been able to name last night, settled in his groin. The throb of reaction was almost painful. Making it impossible for him to ignore it any longer. Or what it implied.

He was physically attracted to his uninvited house guest.

This wasn't just awareness, of her as a woman. It wasn't even the sexual appetite he had always been able to satisfy by masturbating whenever he felt the primal, basic and entirely natural urge to have sex. It was more specific than that. It was the desire to capture *her* plump lips and discover her taste. To feel *her* mouth moulding to his. To drive his tongue into the recesses and capture the sobs of *her* arousal. It was the intense longing to glide his palms beneath the hem of the shapeless sweatshirt of his she was wearing, to discover if her skin was as powder soft as it had seemed last night. The need to explore exactly what lay at the juncture of those long, toned thighs. The yearning to bare her body and caress every part of it.

He had never felt such desires before now—on the rare occasions he had encountered other women.

But somehow worse than his shocking reaction to this woman was the unprecedented urge to believe she was sincere. That if he asked her to, she really would keep his secrets safe.

He ground his teeth together, aware of the sweat sliding down his back. He unfolded his arms, the riot of sensations making him fidgety and tense. He shoved his fists into the pockets of his sweatpants.

The battle to draw himself back from the edge— not to let her see or even sense the yearning driving him—was harder than any battle he had fought in a while.

Surely this was precisely why he had kept himself away from other people for so long. So that he would never feel this driving need to touch, to hold? Because he knew he could not trust anyone to know his needs.

But he couldn't detach his gaze from hers as he noticed the way her eyes darkened.

She was no more immune to these sensations than he was—which only made this situation more untenable, more volatile.

He turned back to the sketches for his new piece, tried to concentrate on them and block out the yearning starting to claw at his gut.

'No camera,' he said, in answer to the question he had managed to grasp in her stream of consciousness. He picked up the pencil. 'Now leave.'

He heard her outraged gasp. But as he began to flesh out the wings of the eagle in the sketches for the new project, he waited to hear the sound of her retreating footsteps. They didn't come.

Her voice, when she spoke again, had a steely quality he had to admire.

'Congratulations, fella, you've just earned the title of the rudest eejit I've ever met. And I worked in a backpackers' pub in Temple Bar for two years.'

His breathing released as he finally heard the pad of her footsteps retreating. The door to the workshop slammed shut. He shouldn't turn around, shouldn't look, but he couldn't seem to stop himself. He tracked her through the glass walkway as she made her way back to the main house. His gaze devoured the sight of her through the swirling snow as she strode away—her head held high, her long legs eating up the ground—before she disappeared down the steps to the basement complex.

He threw down the pencil, the hunger surging through his veins.

He was unlikely to get much work done today. And from the look of the storm, which had been building all morning, they were going to be trapped together in the house for at least another twenty-four hours.

He frowned, annoyed all over again, as the unwanted desire continued to pump into his groin like wildfire. He thrust impatient fingers through his hair then glanced down at the prominent ridge in his sweatpants. He flattened his palm against the strident erection, to rub the rigid flesh through his clothing, furious that she had reduced him to this, and that any relief he found was likely to be temporary—until she was finally gone.

At least the storm would give him a chance to figure out the logistics of getting her back to Saariselkä without risking exposure. But concerns about how to do that took second place to getting her the hell out of his home, so he could control the desperate urge to touch her. Surely the fact that they did not like each other would help?

If last night had felt like the longest night of his life, the next twenty-four hours were going to feel like several hundred years.

CHAPTER FOUR

'WHAT ARE YOU DOING?'

Cara turned from the stove, to see her reluctant host staring at her.

Surprise, surprise, he did not look pleased to see her in his kitchen.

She sighed and placed the wooden spoon on the counter, then brushed her palms on the tea towel she had tucked into the waistband of her leggings.

'Making us supper,' she said, trying to push her lips into some semblance of a smile.

Not easy when he was glaring at her again. But this time, she was prepared for that hard, intense, judgmental look. And determined not to let it
get to her.

She'd managed to find breakfast then taken a long nap in what she now considered to be her bedroom in the huge house. After that, she'd gone to check on her reluctant host. Once she'd ensured he was still ensconced in his workshop, she'd gone exploring.

The house had three levels and was scrupulously clean and tidy throughout. Almost as if no one lived here. There was a library full of books, in a number of different languages, all of them dog-eared and well read. She hadn't managed to find anywhere to charge her dead phone, nor had she found any computer equipment. Which was just odd. Who lived so far from civilisation without benefit of the Internet? What did he do all day apart from read and work on his sculptures, and exercise? And how did he keep the house so clean, unless of course he had staff? But somehow she doubted that, because there was no evidence of anyone else ever having been here. And she'd noticed some kind of device busy remotely vacuuming the front parlour.

The storm had continued to rage outside for the entire day, until night had fallen about two hours ago in the middle of the afternoon.

Mr Grumpy had remained locked in his workshop the whole time. Maybe he had grabbed something to eat earlier while she'd been sleeping, but when she'd found a pantry just off the kitchen and a cold room full of frozen meat and fish, she'd had a brainwave.

She'd tried the stick. It hadn't even put a dent in his determination to think the worst of her. So now she was going to try the carrot. Or rather the carrots, onions, leeks, potatoes, cabbage and meat of her mammy's famous Irish stew, with a small twist, because the only unfrozen meat she'd found in the cold room were reindeer steaks.

For a moment, he was completely nonplussed by her statement. And she felt a strange pang in her chest. Not only did he appear to live here entirely alone, but she would hazard a guess no one had offered to cook him supper in a very long time.

Why that would make her feel momentarily sad for him she had no idea—given that the man practically had *Loner and Proud of It* tattooed across his forehead—but it did.

As much as she'd found her three older brothers a trial during her teenage years, because they'd always had their noses in her business, she had missed the energy and companionship of her big boisterous family once she had decided to set out alone to find her joy as a photographer. It was one thing about her chosen profession she could admit now she regretted—that she hadn't had the time to return to Wexford and visit for over a year.

He cocked his head to one side, staring at the pot she had bubbling on the stove. Then that silvery blue gaze connected with hers again.

'Why?' he asked, sounding not just suspicious now but also confused.

Her lips lifted, the forced smile becoming genuine. There was definitely something to be said for having this man at a disadvantage.

'Because I'm famished and I figured you would be, too. I made what I suspect is probably the first ever Irish Reindeer Stew with the supplies in the pantry.'

He didn't respond, so she felt compelled to fill the void. Conversation, after all, was another of her Celtic superpowers.

'Reindeer's a nice lean meat, it might even work better than the mutton my mammy uses from the farm for hers. But it's basically the same recipe. I couldn't figure out how to work your oven, so I had to slow cook it on the stove but it's—'

'Stop talking.' He held up a hand, cutting her off in mid-flow, his expression pained.

Disappointment rippled through her at his rudeness. But she tried not to take it personally. From the location of his home and his taciturn behaviour so far, she suspected Logan Colton was not a man well versed in conversation. Or any social graces at all really.

After years spent in the company of Irish men—who tended to use great *craic* like a weapon, to charm unsuspecting women—this man's bluntness was almost refreshing.

'I did not ask you to cook for me,' he said, the brittle cynicism back, but it was more wary than accusatory now.

Progress, after a fashion.

'Consider it payback, for saving my life yesterday,' she said, because it was clear he was uncomfortable with being in her debt—and she wanted him to know how ridiculous that was, given what she owed him.

His brow furrowed, as if he was searching for the trap.

She sighed.

Okay, they were really going to have to work on his suspicious nature. But when her stomach growled, she decided that would have to wait.

Switching off the burner under the pot, she set about ladling generous helpings of the stew into two big wooden bowls. He was still standing silently, observing her as if she were a science experiment he couldn't quite figure out. She walked out of the kitchen area with the food, then placed the bowls on the large table already set with cutlery and napkins and an array of pickles and condiments she'd found in the pantry. Like the rest of the house, the kitchen space had a huge picture window that looked out on the forest gorge that dropped below this side of the house. But in the darkness, the large space felt strangely intimate. Especially as she'd had to light a couple of candles on the table when she had been unable to figure out how to turn on the lights in the dining area.

Something she was now regretting, big-time. What on earth had made her think candles would be a good look?

Seriously, Cara? He probably thinks you're trying to seduce him now.

She'd also found a wine cellar. And had uncorked a bottle of merlot, which sat on the table now like another great big red flag to her bad intentions.

Heat flushed into her cheeks as her gaze connected with his.

'I'm sorry. I couldn't find a switch to turn on the lights over here when it got dark.' Luckily the lights in the kitchen had already been on.

'The house's systems are voice activated,' he supplied. 'In Finnish.'

'Grand,' she managed, feeling about as transparent as a new bride's negligee.

Yeah, maybe don't think about naked brides right now.

'That would explain why there wasn't a switch,

then,' she said with a false cheeriness in her voice that made her feel like even more of a fraud.

To her surprise though, he didn't order the lights on. Instead, he came to the table and sat opposite her. If he thought she had been trying to seduce him with the candlelit supper, he didn't let on.

She pushed one full bowl across the table towards him, but drew her hand back sharply when his fingertips brushed hers. The frisson of energy that darted into her abdomen was not helpful at all. His gaze locked on hers momentarily. Had he felt it too? But then he bent his head and began to shovel the stew into his mouth without preamble.

She stared at the way the candlelight flickered over his features and made his tawny hair glow, highlighting a few golden strands in the burnished brown. The candlelight only made him look more rugged and handsome than he had that morning. His heavy stubble had grown into the beginnings of a beard, casting a dark shadow over that hard jaw.

She forced herself to stop staring and start eating.

The stew was rich and tasty—reindeer meat made a great substitute for mutton, who knew?—but she hadn't managed to swallow more than a few bites before she felt full. Eventually, the jumping beans having a rave in her belly made it impossible to eat another bite. Dawdling over her own meal, she took the opportunity to watch him eat unobserved—and the fascination with him, which had increased while she explored his luxurious but strangely impersonal home, grew.

He was methodical but also voracious as he chewed

and swallowed, drawing her gaze to the tanned column of his throat. She noticed the paler skin below the neckline, the chest hair visible past the open collar of his thermal shirt. There was a small crescent-shaped scar high on his right cheekbone, just above his beard, another that slashed through his left eyebrow, and a slight bump on the bridge of his nose. Had he broken it at some point? There were nicks and cuts, some healed, some fresh, on his fingers as he handled the spoon with casual efficiency.

Despite his wealth, it seemed this man hadn't lived a charmed life.

His staggeringly beautiful home seemed to have all the mod cons and then some, but even so, it had to be dangerous, living so far out in the Arctic Circle all on your own.

Why had he hidden himself away in such a remote location? She'd racked her brains all day, trying to remember the details of Logan Coltan's story, which Issi had told her months ago during one of their breaks. She had a vague recollection of a tragedy—surrounding his parents' deaths when he'd been a boy… And the huge fortune in the US—built on his great-grandfather's wealth as some kind of railway baron—which he had become the sole heir to… But nothing more.

Why had he disappeared from the world, and built his very own Fortress? Rather than taking his place as the only surviving member of the Colton dynasty?

The compassion she'd felt earlier pressed against her chest. But surely, it would be foolish to feel sympathy for this hard man, as his solitary life appeared to be one he had not only chosen, but guarded zealously. Even so she couldn't help wondering what could possibly have happened to him to make him choose to starve himself of human companionship so completely.

Who did that?

He placed the spoon abruptly in the bowl, then his head rose. And she found herself trapped in that laser-sharp gaze again, caught staring at him.

The intensity in his expression unnerved her, making her hopelessly aware of the sensations pulsing under her skin.

But she refused to detach her gaze from his or feel guilty for watching him.

She lifted the bottle of wine and poured herself a generous glass. She wasn't a big drinker but right now she needed something to calm nerves that were fizzing and sparking and doing nothing to cool the hot weight in her belly.

She took a hasty gulp, then finally found her manners. 'Would you like a glass of your own wine?'

He seemed to consider the question then gave a slight dip of his head.

I'll take that as a yes.

She filled his glass. He took a sip of the fruity wine, continuing to watch her unabashed over the rim, but as usual he felt no need to fill the silence.

Unlike her.

'Was it all right?' She nodded towards his empty bowl. 'The stew?'

'Yes.' His husky voice seemed to scrape over her skin in the semi-darkness.

'That's grand. I'm glad you enjoyed it,' she said, then forced herself to shut up.

But so many questions burned on her tongue. Questions that had been swirling in her head all day like the storm outside as she'd discovered what she could about him from his home. The silence seemed to build in intensity, throbbing between them—not unlike the hot weight in her abdomen. Eventually she couldn't prevent herself from asking the most pressing one.

'Do you live here entirely alone?'

His eyes narrowed, the familiar cynicism making the pale blue of his irises look even more steely than usual. And she immediately wished she could grab the question back. She didn't want to ruin the truce she'd worked so hard to earn.

'Forget I asked,' she said.

At exactly the same time as he said, 'Yes.'

She blinked, surprised he had given her an answer. She already knew that he had never been seen in Saariselkä, which was Finland's northernmost town, and had to be well over fifty miles to the south if her calculations were correct. How did he even get his supplies?

She knew she really shouldn't push her luck, but the next question spilled out regardless. 'Don't you get lonely? Being so far from civilisation?'

His brows rose, as if the question made no sense to him. 'No.'

But then his gaze raked over her face, the penetrating look one that had her cheeks burning. And she had the weird sensation that even though he had told her the truth, he might not be entirely sure of his answer. Awareness—and that tangible spark of attraction she had felt when his fingers had brushed hers on the bowl—sizzled in the air between them.

She swallowed, her throat suddenly dry. But she couldn't seem to control the brutal pulse of awareness. His eyes darkened as his gaze dropped to her mouth. She licked her lips, feeling his perusal like a physical caress.

What was he thinking? Surely, he must be able to feel it, too? Whatever *it* was… Because she'd never felt like this before… Certainly never had to struggle to control her response to a man.

And if it was desire, what on earth were they supposed to do about it?

She jumped up, suddenly desperate to break the tension. But as she went to lift his empty bowl, intending to load it into the state-of-the-art dishwasher, he snagged her wrist.

Sensation pulsed and flared, the hot rock between her thighs becoming molten as their gazes locked again.

'Stay out of my way,' he murmured, the hard line of his jaw and the dark arousal in his eyes making it clear he was holding on to his control with an effort.

He dropped her hand, then stood and left the room.

She watched him go, mesmerised by the muscular grace of his movements as he stalked away. The flash of memory blindsided her. He reminded her of an Arctic wolf—the leader of a marauding pack—that she had photographed a month ago. That wolf had been predatory, deadly, dangerous, but also staggeringly beautiful in its ruthless pursuit of its prey. She rubbed her wrist where the skin still burned from his touch.

His warning had been blunt and unequivocal, just like everything else about him. But it had also answered the question that had been hanging in the air between them during their meal.

He felt this devastating chemical reaction too.

The throb of arousal in her gut pounded harder, reckless and dangerous and like nothing she had ever felt before. The liquid heat settled, wedging itself between her thighs like a hot brick. Adrenaline surged, and an excitement she'd only ever felt for her work before now charged through her veins—reckless and intoxicating.

While she tidied away their bowls and cleaned up the kitchen, she tried to talk some sense into herself. And ignore the relentless pulse of desire.

She should do as he suggested. Avoid him. The house was big enough that they didn't need to cross paths at all—and surely the storm would clear by morning. But she couldn't shake the thought that the livewire sexual connection they shared was even more disturbing to him than it was to her.

She was playing with fire, she understood that. But there was something so raw and vibrant about this man, and she had always been drawn to the wild, the untamed… Which was precisely why she had made a career out of observing and capturing them on film.

Logan Colton was an enigma. A fascinating, compelling enigma. And imagining what it would be like to unleash the raw sexual energy she sensed pulsed just beneath the surface of that cast-iron control was as unbearably exciting as it was unsettling.

He'd told her to keep her distance. Made it clear he wanted nothing to do with her. Just as he seemed to want to have nothing to do with the outside world.

But she knew the truth was a great deal more complex. Logan had needs, just like any man. Or woman for that matter. Needs she suspected he had been denying for a very long time—or he wouldn't be living out in the Arctic Circle entirely alone.

Needs that she could admit now she'd always denied too.

He had warned her off because he didn't want his control challenged. Didn't want to acknowledge this attraction.

But unfortunately, she'd never been very good at following orders. Especially orders imposed on her by other people. Just ask her mammy.

And she'd never been scared to pursue the things that fascinated and excited her.

And at the moment, the thing that fascinated and excited her the most was him.

CHAPTER FIVE

Standing at the end of the jetty he had built two summers ago over the lake, Logan unfolded the long serrated blade. He began to saw through the ice to recreate the swimming hole that had frozen over during the storm.

He grunted in frustration as he shoved the blade into the ice.

He would not be able to take his unwanted guest to her vehicle now until tomorrow, as it would be dark again in only a few hours. He had worked out a plan to take her to the broken snowmobile, check the photos on her camera, and then let her call for rescue. If he left her in the forest clearing before rescue arrived he would not need to compromise his privacy. Without a working GPS she would never be able to find her way back through the forest to his home. But his plan had been thrown into turmoil today, because the storm had continued to rage all morning. It would take over an hour to get to her vehicle, and he could hardly leave her alone in the forest after dark.

Blast her.

He breathed through his annoyance. He had avoided her so far today and left her a note explaining the situation, so she would continue to stay away from him until they could leave at first light tomorrow. But getting out of the house had seemed the best solution today after he had found her cooking them supper last night.

He should not have accepted the peace offering—even though the stew had been delicious. He was still furious with the foolish decision and the weakness that had caused it, that visceral spurt of yearning to stay… With her.

He would not make the same mistake twice, which meant heeding his own warning, and staying away from her too.

The late morning sunlight made the freshly fallen snow sparkle and warmed his exposed skin. He preferred to use the traditional hand tools for this job. It was hard, sweaty work, but it reminded him of his grandfather—and provided a useful and much-needed distraction from the confusing thoughts and feelings that had been consuming him for twenty-four hours now.

He had already spent half an hour drilling the four corners of the hole into the ice, using a hand-powered drill, but it was the saw work that was the most tiring.

His muscles warmed as he segmented the square hole into two triangular blocks then stepped on each one in turn to dislodge them. Eventually, after much careful pressure he was able to employ the pick to lever the ice blocks under the edge of the hole. Then he dropped the ladder and fixed it to the ice.

Ice swimming was a three-hundred-year-old Finnish tradition, which he'd happily embraced as a teenager at his grandfather's instigation to help quell the night terrors. It was dangerous to swim on your own, but he had no qualms about having the brief dip whenever the weather allowed. It alleviated any stress in his life and unblocked his creativity when it stalled if he was feeling low. Or extremely frustrated.

Like now.

Because he would be forced to endure another night with *her* in his home.

Luckily the woman—whose name he had been careful not to ask—had stayed out of his way this morning. *Good*, he was glad she had listened for once.

That he had woken up after last night's meal with a strident erection had only frustrated him more.

It wasn't the first time he'd had erotic dreams. He was a grown man after all. But it was the first time those dreams had had a face, and a sultry spicy scent, and striking emerald eyes—the gold shards in the irises spellbound with arousal—that had bored into his soul. And made every one of his pulse points pound.

Stop thinking about her. Damn it.

At last, the *avanto* was ready. He stalked back to the cabin on the edge of the lake to prepare for his swim. After feeding more logs onto the fire that heated the cabin's sauna, he stripped down to his shorts and stepped inside. The dry heat relaxed tired muscles, while the sweat cleansed his pores and helped to clear his head of the many inconvenient thoughts… Of her. After ten minutes, he crossed the jetty and took the steps into the icy lake.

The water—its temperature hovering just above freezing—felt like sharp needles digging into his skin, but as he swam across the hole, adrenaline surged, bursting into his brain and dislodging the frustration.

The endorphins built to a wave as he climbed out and headed across the snowy dock in his shorts and a pair of sliders to protect his bare feet from the ice. But as he reached the sauna cabin, the cold rushing over his skin and making every nerve ending tingle with life and vitality, he heard a staggered breath. His head jerked up, and he spotted the woman who had been haunting his thoughts standing under the trees, wrapped up against the cold, her gaze roaming over his virtually naked body.

He swore abruptly, then clasped his arms around his torso. The frigid cold numbed his skin, but did nothing for the heat that blasted back into his gut.

Had she been watching him, swimming? And why did that only make the hunger worse?

Dislodging his gaze with an effort, before he froze to death, he stalked towards the sauna and ducked inside. Even though the last damn thing he needed was more heat.

She hadn't listened. Why was he even surprised?

As he doused the hot coals with lake water, the blast of steam hit his skin and the adrenaline rush from the cold-water immersion morphed into something a great deal more dangerous.

The arousal he'd been intending to dampen flared back to life. As he settled onto the sauna's pine bench, thoughts of her invaded his senses. Those full lips pressed to his chest, skating over his belly, surrounding his... The yearning to be touched by another human being, to be caressed by *her*, became so intense, the ache built until it became unbearable.

He swore viciously—unable to focus now with her so close, and unable to find another temporary release because it would only make him more ashamed of his weakness where she was concerned.

He stepped out of the steam-filled hut and got dressed in the cooler air of the outer cabin. When he stepped outside, she was no longer there. No longer watching.

The ripple of disappointment disturbed him, but not as much as the feel of her gaze rioting over his skin that still lingered, making the ache flare anew.

As he trudged through the forest, he found her footprints in the snow. And followed them back to the house.

But when he saw her through the kitchen's picture window, he detoured towards his workshop.

She had invaded his privacy, but worse, she had turned the solitude that he had enjoyed for so long—and relied on to make him whole—into something problematic, something not enough.

'Don't you get lonely?'

The question she'd asked last night pushed against his consciousness, opening a hollow space in his gut. He'd never been lonely. He embraced the quiet, had always loved being self-sufficient and self-contained, had never had any need for companionship or conversation—not since his grandfather had died.

But he couldn't shake the thought that there was something fundamental missing from his life now.

And that was her fault.

He tried to control the frustration and anger as he headed to his workshop. But as he selected the wood for his next project, it refused to fade. He picked up the different pieces that he had foraged for in the forest during the long summer days. But as he assessed the grain, tested for faults and knots that might ruin the design he had sketched, he imagined touching her skin. And wondered what it would feel like under his fingers. Those toned muscles, the soft contours of her body, her high full breasts, the taut nipples visible through the clinging fabric of her thermal undershirt…

The urge to make her gasp as she had in the forest, or shudder as she had when their fingers had brushed the night before, became desperate and demanding.

He dumped the chunk of silver pine he had been assessing back into the basket.

Swearing viciously, he stalked out of his workshop. Avoiding her wasn't going to work, because she had refused to avoid him. Which meant they would both have to face the consequences now. Once and for all.

'Why did you spy on me?'

Cara glanced up from her breakfast to find her irate

host standing over her. She'd seen him marching past the kitchen earlier to head to his workshop.

Guilt wrapped around her throat, making it hard for her to swallow down the spoonful of berries and yoghurt he'd caught her eating.

Accusation and anger shone in his eyes, turning the pale blue to a fierce steel.

'I—I didn't…'

She hadn't followed him intentionally. She'd read his curt note that morning, informing her they would leave at first light tomorrow—and also understood what he hadn't said, that he expected her to remain invisible until then.

She'd bristled at the commanding tone, but had been determined to control the reckless thoughts from last night—when she'd seriously contemplated acting on the passion that flared between them.

Because that was madness.

But when the storm had died, the shimmering white had beckoned her out into the quiet wilderness. She hadn't been able to resist the urge to get dressed in the clothing she'd found washed and folded in the laundry room off the garage.

She had ventured out to explore the land, on the pretext of figuring out if any of it was familiar. Maybe they weren't that far from the national forest where she'd left the snowmobile? After all, she'd been delirious the evening he'd brought her here, maybe the ride hadn't been as long as she'd assumed. But nothing had looked remotely familiar—the mountain gorge behind the house and the thick forest beyond a far cry from the frozen boreal forest of the tundra where she'd been tracking the lynx.

Changing tack, and mindful of not straying too far from the house, she'd been doubling back through the spruce and birch trees when she had spotted his tracks on the north side of the building. Without questioning the impulse, she'd followed his large footprints in the newly fallen snow until she had seen him through the trees busy sawing a hole in the icy lake beside a small wooden cabin.

She'd watched him work, becoming aware of what he was doing—because she had heard of the Finnish tradition of ice swimming in the resort in Saariselkä. She'd never tried it herself. But still she'd been fascinated by the methodical way he used the old-fashioned hand tools. The strength in his arms and shoulders— even visible beneath the heavy clothing—had drawn her to him as he'd finished creating the swimming hole. She'd been spellbound. And then he'd disappeared into the cabin. And come out a few minutes later virtually naked.

It was only then, as her pulse rate rocketed and the awareness in her gut flared like a firework, that she had acknowledged what she'd really been waiting to see—like the worst kind of voyeur.

His pale skin had been pink from the heat, the steam rising off those broad shoulders and long legs. Her gaze had devoured the defined ridges of his six-pack, the line of hair that tapered down from the light fleece that covered his pecs through washboard abs. As he'd stood at the ladder for several seconds, stretching and flexing before climbing in, she'd became fascinated by the way the damp shorts moulded to his backside framing a truly magnificent set of glutes.

He seemed immune to the cold, which was beginning to make her fingers numb and her eyelashes freeze in six layers of clothing, after standing still for too long spying on him.

The fervent wish that she'd had her camera equipment had consumed her. She would have loved to capture him on film as he lowered his body into the lake, his tall, broad frame somehow at one with the frozen beauty of his surroundings.

But once he'd been immersed to his neck in the freezing water, a rush of panic and fear had all but crippled her as she had waited what felt like several eternities for him to climb out again.

Wasn't it dangerous to swim alone, out here in the wilderness, miles from anywhere? Did he do this often? How could he be so reckless with his personal safety?

The fear and indignation returned in a rush as he stood over her now, thankfully masking her guilt and quelling the blush that threatened to incinerate her.

'I wasn't spying on you...'

Or not much, she told herself staunchly.

'I was making sure you didn't die.'

The dark frown became catastrophic. 'What?'

'You were ice swimming alone. That's dangerous. Even I know that and I'm not even Finnish, I'm Irish,' she added, warming to her theme as she began to babble. 'I've been living in Lapland for over six months.

And I happen to know it's not safe to ice swim without back-up. If you'd had a pulmonary oedema while you were in there you could have become disorientated and there would have been no one to pull you out. I was just being your back-up.'

Getting an eyeful of his impressive physique and the way his bare body pulsed with vitality in the bright Arctic daylight had been a coincidental fringe benefit.

'My safety is not your concern,' he said, his firm lips pursing into a thin line, that steel-blue gaze going a little squinty with frustration.

Join the club, fella.

'Of course it is. You saved my life,' she said, becoming exasperated now with his rampant individualism. 'I owe you.'

'You owe me nothing.' He planted his palms on the table, and leaned over her, no doubt to intimidate her with that arctic glare, but she could see the awareness in his gaze as it swept over her face and dipped towards her breasts, which were moulded against the thin thermal undershirt she'd stripped down to after rushing back to the house. Something cracked open inside her, something raw and passionate. And the fierce feeling of connection—which she had been trying to deny ever since he had first appeared out of the storm like an avenging angel—careered through her body.

'There is nothing I need from you,' he added, his tone brittle with determination. 'Nothing I need from anyone.'

But she knew it wasn't entirely true, when his gaze

swept over her again—and she saw the fierce hunger he couldn't hide.

She jumped to her feet, knocking her chair onto the floor. And stalked around the table, until they were toe to toe—possessed by a desire she had tried to deny all through the night.

He straightened, shifting away from her as she invaded his personal space. But the desire in her veins intensified, becoming hot and fluid and unstoppable.

'You're lying,' she whispered. Then she did what she had dreamed of doing all night. She placed her palm on his cheek, to soothe the rigid line of his jaw.

He grunted, the muscles tensing beneath her hand, as if he had been burned—not unlike his reaction the first time she had touched him—but this time, he didn't pull away. Instead, he closed his eyes, his breathing ragged as if he needed a moment to absorb the shock. When he opened his eyes again, what she saw had her breath seizing in her lungs.

Raw visceral need.

She ran her thumb across his lips, felt the firm line tremble, and became mesmerised as her own breathing accelerated to match the harsh murmur of his.

His pupils dilated, the vibrant steel in his gaze darkening to black, and she sensed the effort it was taking him to remain still.

So she went with her gut to break the deadlock.

'Can I kiss you, Logan?' she asked.

She saw the moment his control snapped, like a high-tension wire wound too tight.

He grasped her hips and dragged her against the

unyielding line of his body. The ridge of his erection pressed into her belly as he slanted his mouth across hers—and gave her his answer.

His kiss was firm, deliberate, possessing her mouth as his tongue thrust deep, and duelled with hers in furious strokes, but it was the edge of desperation—so raw, so basic, so elemental and unskilled—that had the need pulsing at her core.

She grasped his head, threaded her fingers through his long hair, and opened her mouth to take more of those eager, untutored thrusts.

Consumed by passion, she sobbed, when he ripped his mouth free and pressed his forehead to hers. She could feel the shiver of reaction coursing through his body, or was it hers?

'I want you.' The words seemed to be torn from his throat—like a curse.

She released the fingers she had fisted in his hair, to press her palms to his hard cheeks and lift his head to stare into his eyes.

So many emotions swirled in the pale blue depths— desire, longing, but most of all baffled desperation.

This was madness. He didn't even know her name, because he hadn't bothered to ask. And she knew a part of him still did not want her in his home. A *large* part of him. But something about the desperation she could see in his face echoed in her heart—and called to her own loneliness. Her own denial.

She'd never truly wanted a man before. Always scared to take the risk. Scared she might end up like her mammy, tied to a brute like her father.

But this wasn't about affection, this was all about desire and chemistry. She'd never felt this rush of endorphins, of excitement and exhilaration. And she might never feel it again, because she already knew how rare it was, after too many botched and aborted make-out sessions as a teenager.

She'd been determined to be smart, sensible, in charge of her own destiny, always. But had she secretly also been holding out, hoping to feel the sensations she'd heard other women talk about? Sensations she had convinced herself might not exist for her.

And now she knew they did.

Why shouldn't they enjoy each other? If they were both willing? And they both needed it?

She had nearly died two days ago. What if he hadn't answered her Mayday, and she had perished out there in the frozen forest, a virgin? Having never known what it was to experience physical pleasure? Life wasn't guaranteed, she'd found that out while she huddled in that snowdrift praying for rescue.

And, to be fair, he *had* saved her life. And nursed her through the night. For all that he didn't like her.

However surly and uncommunicative he was, he had a core of honesty, of integrity, that made her sure she could trust him, with this much at least.

Ah, to hell with it. Stop overthinking this. Just do it already, Cara. This might be your only chance.

She kept her gaze fixed on his, threaded her fingers back into his hair, yanked his mouth back to hers. And told him the truth.

'I want you too,' she whispered against his lips, before licking across the seam, demanding entry.

His guttural moan made her feel powerful in a way she never had before.

This time, she took control of the kiss, thrusting her tongue deep into his mouth. Licking and sucking as he let her lead.

They devoured each other, but as they came up for air a second time, she knew it wasn't enough. Not to satisfy the ache building at her core.

His hands had remained on her hips, the tremble of reaction suggesting he was using the last threads of his control to keep them there.

She took one of his large hands and placed it firmly on her backside.

He shuddered, his fingers tensing and releasing as he stroked the firm flesh. Then he slanted his lips across hers and lifted her into another all-consuming kiss.

It seemed to take an eternity, but eventually he took the hint and slid one large palm beneath the waistband of her sweatpants and panties. His callused fingers rasped across her aching flesh, his moans matching her sobs as he pressed his palm to her vulva.

Her need soared, flooding her panties with moisture.

He found the sodden folds, then stepped back abruptly, yanking his hand out of her underwear. His gaze was fierce on hers and full of—what was that, exactly? Because it looked like a combination of awe and astonishment.

'You like my touch?' he rasped, his breathing ragged.

Why did he look so surprised? And why did that only make the hot weight between her legs rise to squeeze around her ribs?

She nodded, because he seemed to need an answer. 'Yes. I love having your hands on me.'

As he continued to stare at her, the heat from her core rose to burn her collarbone.

But before she could become embarrassed by her own enthusiasm, his gaze sank to her breasts. He cradled her neck, his touch firm again, and possessive, his gaze fierce as it roamed over the tight nipples clearly visible through the thin undershirt. But again, he hesitated.

The moment might have been awkward. She'd never met a man who hadn't wanted to take the initiative, especially as she had made it so clear she wanted him. But something about his reticence felt empowering.

Why not take the initiative yourself, Cara?

She grabbed the hem of her thermal undershirt and stripped it off over her head. His gaze narrowed, scalding her skin, the approval in his eyes almost as breathtaking as the desire.

She fumbled around for the back hook on her bra. How did you do this sort of thing gracefully? But it was clear she didn't need to worry about looking seductive. Because his gaze was riveted to her as she finally managed to discard the scrap of lace.

His face lifted to hers, awareness lighting his cheeks, the fire in his eyes turning them to a bright silver. It was all the validation she needed.

He appeared to be holding his breath. Then his lungs released, and he ran his tongue over his bottom lip.

'You are beautiful,' he said, his tone thick with reverence, his gaze rich with fascination.

And she felt truly beautiful for the first time in her life.

Her nipples hardened, elongating under that intense gaze. He lifted his hand, his expression reverent as he ran his thumb under the rigid peak.

Her own breath guttered out in an audible sob.

He paused, but didn't drop his hand, then he began to explore in earnest. His touch was careful and patient but full of purpose as he grazed the nipple with his thumb, lifted the weight in his palm, circled the areola in a methodical but profoundly sensual caress.

He watched her intently as the vice tightened at her core, the ache becoming painful.

She shuddered, the desire pouring between her thighs as he bent to lick the peak at last. He worked one nipple, then the other, sucking and tugging, making the arrows of pleasure dart to her core.

She felt trapped by her own desire, the insistent caresses, his determined touch reminding her of his long strong fingers on the pencil as he sketched in his workshop… Or his competent hands on the traditional tools at the lake. She grasped his head, her own dropping back, her body so alive with sensation she was struggling to breathe.

She'd never realised her breasts were so sensitive,

but she could feel the pressure building at her core.
Insistent. Incendiary. Shockingly intense.

It wasn't enough to take her over though, not quite,
and being suspended on the knife edge of release soon
felt like torture.

'Please… Touch me more.'

His head lifted. 'How? Where?'

Again, she was momentarily nonplussed. How
could he seem so competent, so hot and yet also not
know how to touch her?

But then the desperation gripped her, and, grasping
his hand, she shoved it back into her panties. He didn't
need any more instruction, his blunt fingers finding
the hot nub throbbing between her thighs.

She shuddered, and tensed as he circled, teased,
then glided one callused forefinger right over the heart
of her.

She bucked as he worked the spot ruthlessly—
rubbing, touching, claiming, branding. She gripped
his shoulders, riding his hand now, the orgasm so
close…

She felt wild, wanton, and she didn't care, because
it felt so, *so* good. He thrust one long finger inside her,
then two, stretching her tight flesh unbearably, while
still working her clitoris ruthlessly with his thumb.

'Oh… Yes.' She directed him, even though he
seemed to know instinctively just how to touch her
to drive her insane. 'Right…there…'

The powerful rush of pleasure burst over her at last,
sending her senses reeling as she tumbled into a hot

vat of pure bliss. He continued to stroke her through the vicious climax until she was limp and shaking.

She grasped his wrist, too sensitive to stand more.

'Please... I can't... It's too much.'

His fingers stilled, and he drew his hand from her panties.

She heard his rough chuckle and opened her eyes to see him sucking his fingers.

'Delicious,' he murmured.

She blushed, stunned by the renewed pulse of desire. The fierce approval in his gaze made her feel like a goddess.

'You are more beautiful when you come,' he said.

The words—thick with passion—seemed somehow incongruously poetic coming from this unsentimental and uncommunicative man.

Her body felt limp, sated, and strangely enervated. Her heart hammered her ribs.

The smile on his lips stunned her a little. She'd never seen him smile, hadn't imagined it was possible for him to be more handsome, more compelling. But the slight twist of his lips and the triumphant gleam in his eyes were as stunningly beautiful as the frozen landscape he lived in.

That would be the afterglow talking, Cara, you dolt.

She tried to talk some sense into herself, but with the endorphins still charging through her system, it wasn't easy.

'We should find a bed,' she managed.

'You wish to come again?' His eyebrows lifted, the surprise on his face making her laugh.

Good Lord. How could he be both scarily intense and stupidly adorable at one and the same time?

The man was an enigma and no mistake. An enigma she couldn't wait to figure out.

She cradled the heavy erection stretching the front of his sweatpants, feeling bold now with her new-found experience. She assessed the heft and weight of him—which were…*impressive*.

'Yes, but with you inside me this time,' she managed.

He tensed, but she could feel the erection strain against her palm.

He'd given her more pleasure than she had imagined possible and she wanted desperately to return the favour.

He grunted, but then nodded. 'Okay.'

Before she could protest, he dislodged her hand and scooped her into his arms.

She let out a shriek of shock and delight as she found herself being carried up the wide stairs leading to the house's top level. She knew she wasn't particularly heavy, but it was as if she weighed nothing at all.

Her laughter died as they entered an enormous room at the far end of the house.

Three walls were made of glass with a wide bed in the centre of it.

The breathtaking vista of forest and mountains beyond the glass stretched to the horizon, as the dying sunlight poured into the expertly appointed room giving it an eerily beautiful glow.

She'd made a point of not exploring the upstairs when she'd been checking out the house yesterday. But as he set her on her feet, she wished she had seen this room before. Because it might have helped to control the lump of emotion burning in her throat as he stripped off in front of her.

Moments later he stood before her naked—his strong body so much harder and firmer than hers.

'Your house is stunning,' she whispered, to cover what she suspected was her awestruck expression.

'Not as stunning as you,' he murmured.

She clasped her arms over her naked breasts, suddenly self-conscious at how she'd fallen apart so spectacularly at his touch. How was she going to return the favour when she knew nothing at all about pleasuring a guy?

He was magnificent. In every way. Not just the rough-hewn features, the muscular torso and long legs dusted with hair, but also the thick erection thrusting proudly from the nest of dark hair at his groin.

For a moment she couldn't seem to take her eyes off it. She swallowed past the rawness in her throat.

Oh... My...

'That's... It's... You're very...large,' she stammered, finally managing to finish the sentence while feeling both turned on and ridiculously gauche.

Sheesh, Cara, awkward much?

She'd promised him a temptress but was actually an untried virgin. What little sexual experience she'd had as a teenager had not been the best. And had certainly never been worth risking her father's wrath. She could still remember the awful fallout from her Debs—the Irish prom—when she'd returned home with her date an hour after curfew. Her father had branded her a whore and her mother had given her a lecture on where babies came from—as if she didn't already know that. But after that grubby, rushed and unsatisfying make-out session in the back of Barry O'Connell's mother's Skoda, and the names her father had screamed at her afterwards, she'd never had any desire to go further. Until now.

Logan tucked a knuckle under her chin and lifted her face to his.

'Is it too large?'

For a moment, she thought the blunt enquiry might be a boast, but then she registered the concern on his face.

'I don't know,' she replied honestly, feeling more awkward by the second, but no less turned on, weirdly. 'I don't think so.'

Surely in the grand scheme of things he wasn't so big she couldn't accommodate him. After all, his size was as big a turn-on as the rest of him. She pursed her lips, then spewed out the truth.

'It's just, I've never actually gone all the way before— which probably seems mad for a woman past twenty, but it's just...' She trailed off. Was this too much information again? Probably. He hadn't said a word, hadn't even flickered an eyelash at her confession. Was he put off by her lack of experience? Irritated? Annoyed? It was impossible to tell. 'So you'll be needing to take it slowly. Sorry,' she finished.

His brows lowered, but then his gorgeous mouth tilted in a breathtaking—and endearingly self-deprecating—grin. 'I am nearly thirty,' he said. 'And this is my first time, too, with a woman instead of my hand.'

For a moment she wasn't sure she'd heard him correctly. 'You're not serious?' she blurted out. 'You're a virgin?'

How could he have given her the best sexual experience of her life already—be so hot and gorgeous—and be as inexperienced as she was?

The information just wouldn't compute.

The smile on his lips died, his gaze becoming flat and direct. 'This is a problem?'

'No... No. Not at all.'

Wow, way to shove your foot down your own throat, Cara.

The concern had left his eyes, to be replaced by... Well, nothing. The shutters that had been lifted while he'd stroked her to orgasm—and she'd gone completely to bits under his instinctive and assured caresses—had slammed right back down again.

He turned away, lifting his sweatpants off the bed where he'd thrown them.

Panic assailed her. Had he changed his mind? Had she ruined it?

She grasped his arm, felt the ripple of muscle, making her frantic.

'Please, it's not... It's not a problem at all. It's just

really surprising. And flattering,' she said, desperate to stop him from getting dressed again.

He'd never done it before with anyone. And he wanted to do it with her. Why did that suddenly feel like a massively big deal? She suspected his decision had more to do with opportunity than anything else. Just as hers had. Had he ever had a woman here before? Exactly how long had he lived here alone?

But even so, she felt the lump of emotion swell in her throat when he continued to stare at her, and assess her statement, with that blank look on his face—as if his emotions were not for public consumption. Ever.

Maybe he had only picked her because she had literally landed in his lap. And thrown herself at him. But it still made her feel special and important—in a way Barry O'Connell and the other guys she'd kissed as an inquisitive teen never had.

She gulped down the lump still expanding in her throat.

Now, don't go getting ahead of yourself. This is still just endorphins and chemistry and opportunity and sex...

But she was betting sex with Logan Colton— the most accomplished virgin in the northern hemisphere—would be really, really spectacular sex.

As long as she hadn't messed up her chance.

He slung his sweatpants back on the bed—and relief rushed through her. The intense look on his face was unnerving, but she could still see the fierce arousal in his gaze.

And that prodigious erection—which he seemed

remarkably relaxed about—hadn't deflated one bit. That had to be a good sign.

'You are sure?' he said at last.

Her breath released in an audible sigh.

'Yes, I'm totally positive. It's grand.' Her gaze dipped to that gorgeous column of erect flesh—which she suspected no other woman had even seen before her.

'Could I...?' she began, then had to swallow past the newest constriction in her throat.

Oh, for pity's sake, Cara. This is your first time too, and weren't you just after telling him it's not a big deal?

'Can I touch you?' she asked.

He seemed to consider the question. Then nodded. 'Yes.'

She let out a nervous half-laugh, stupidly touched by his total lack of guile.

He didn't seem to be remotely embarrassed by his lack of experience. So why the heck was she?

'That's grand, then,' she said, feeling both strangely euphoric and also oddly moved.

Maybe this wasn't that big a deal to him. But in a lot of ways, it was to her.

Why had she waited so long to have sex? Why had she denied herself this experience?

Maybe because the few intimate encounters she'd had had been fraught with nerves and embarrassment—and marred by the spectre of her father's judgment. But this felt somehow new and different and impossibly exhilarating. Because for the first time ever, it felt as if there was no judgment here. And nothing to prove.

This was all about the elemental attraction between them and nothing more.

And after too many painfully self-conscious encounters in her teens, she found that impossibly liberating.

She sank to her knees in front of him. Then glanced up at his face when he grunted.

His gaze was bold as he threaded his fingers into her hair, caressing her scalp, his expression so full of that fierce yearning she was captivated. And humbled.

She curled her fingers around his hard shaft. A shot of adrenaline reverberated in her core when he shuddered.

He clasped her skull in both hands now, his fingers tensing, kneading. She leant forward, desperate for the taste of him, driven to do something she had never even considered doing before.

She licked the thick length from root to tip, gathering the salty droplet on her eager tongue. The erection jerked forward, as if seeking her touch.

He swore viciously as she kissed the swollen head, adoring the musty taste of him—excitement charged through her veins as he bucked against her lips. And groaned.

As he began to shake, his hips thrusting of their own accord, she opened her mouth as wide as she could manage and worshipped him with it. Determined to give him the glorious release he had given her.

Logan let out a guttural moan, the feel of her lips on his swollen shaft so exquisite it was almost painful.

Watching her beneath him, on her knees, was the most erotic thing he had ever seen in his life, the thought of possessing all of her more than he could stand. The pleasure built at the base of his spine, his palms beginning to sweat as he resisted the powerful urge to thrust harder into her mouth.

He grunted. Tensed.

It was too good. Too much.

He clasped her head and dragged himself free. She stared at him, her eyes dazed with the same lust that burned in his gut.

'I wish to be inside you,' he murmured, his voice so husky it sounded as if it had been wrenched from the depths of his soul.

He hooked clumsy hands under her arms to lift her off her knees. If she stayed down there any longer, he would not be responsible for his actions.

Falling to his own knees, he stripped off her sweatpants, and the thin thermal tights she wore beneath. She clasped his shoulder, her nails digging into his flesh as she struggled to steady herself while he discarded the last of her clothing.

With his head level with her belly he could smell her desire. He licked his lips and sighed. Another time he intended to enjoy feasting on that scent. But right now, he couldn't wait.

He lifted her into his arms, then dropped her—without a lot of finesse—onto the bed.

He took a moment to absorb the sight and imprint it on his memory. Her soft flushed body—her skin glowing in the redolent twilight—lay on the white sheets, her reddish-blonde hair cast in a halo around her head.

'I do not have protection,' he managed around the hunger beginning to claw at his throat as well as his gut.

She seemed dazed for a moment—he knew how she felt—that sparkling green still riveted to his fierce erection. But then her gaze rose to his. 'I… I have a contraceptive implant.' She touched her upper arm and he noticed a small bump under the skin. 'It's to help with my heavy periods, because they used to be so excruciating. It would take me days to recover every month, plus periods are a pain when you're camping in the wild and…' Her soft musical voice babbled to a stop. But what had once annoyed him, captivated him now.

He stared at her, to process the barrage of information.

'I'm sorry, that's probably TMI…' She babbled some more.

He frowned. He had no idea what she meant by this TMI, but it did not matter. Adrenaline surged as his lust-fogged brain finally registered what she had said: he could climax inside her and it would not risk a pregnancy.

He climbed on the bed, his hands clasping her hips to angle her body. He would have preferred to turn her over, to sink himself deep inside her from behind, the desire to hide the effect she had on him instinctive. But he was aware he would need to gauge her reaction. She had seemed concerned about his size and he was her first lover, he did not want to risk hurting her.

But as she clasped his shoulders, and lifted her knees, her body cradling his, giving him better access, her gaze met his and he saw the same deep yearning in her eyes that pulsed so ferociously inside him.

He found her entrance, slid the thick shaft through the swollen folds, to nudge the spot he had found earlier.

She reared back and let out a guttural sob. 'Please, just do it, Logan, before I die of wanting.'

He grunted out a rough chuckle, astonished she could make him laugh when he was about to fall apart.

But he took the hint, and, gripping her hips, lifted her body to his, to find her entrance.

He pressed into the hot flesh. Then stopped abruptly when she flinched, but she shook her head.

'It's okay, keep going, it feels good,' she said, her fingers digging into his shoulder blades.

The feel of her, so tight, so tender, massaging him in spasms, had the last of his breath guttering out of his lungs as he thrust through the slight barrier.

He held himself deep, feeling her stretch to accept him, her pants matching his own harsh breaths.

Had he ever felt anything more exquisite in his life?

The question echoed in his consciousness but was swept away before he could engage with it by the tidal wave of yearning, of desperation as he felt her muscles twitch and pulse along his length, drawing him deeper still. The urge to move became so strong, he had to grit his teeth, to pull out slowly and thrust back as carefully as he could, amazed when he sank even further.

'Is it okay? You are not hurt?' he managed.

She shook her head. 'No, I'm good. You have to move, Logan.'

He didn't need a second invitation, the primal urge already clawing at his spine.

His rhythm was clumsy, uncoordinated at first, but her sighs, her shudders spurred him on. He rotated his hips, pulled out, thrust back, establishing the undulating thrusts, aware of what made her sigh, what made her tense.

The need built like a tsunami, claiming every part of his soul, in sweet, stunning increments, until he couldn't hold back any part of his need.

She clung to him, her nails carving deep grooves in his back, his body rejoicing as the sharp pain combined with the visceral pleasure.

She cried out, her body massaging him at last, and the pleasure exploded. He shouted out as his seed pumped into her—draining him, and shattering her.

He collapsed on top of her, throwing him over into a deep abyss of perfect gratification, pure pleasure, as one last coherent thought echoed inside his head.

I must let her go. Or I will want to do this again... And again... And again. Until I am lost for ever.

CHAPTER SIX

CARA LAY STARING at the vaulted wooden beams that made up the ceiling of Logan Colton's bedroom. His shoulder lay heavy on her chest, pressing her into the mattress.

She'd had two stunning orgasms in Logan's arms. *Two!* And while he still felt huge inside her, and she was a little sore, the glittering pleasure—and that heady feeling of fulfilment—was far greater.

But it wasn't just the endorphins barrelling through her system that were making her heart throb in her chest. She slid her hands over his shoulders, wanting to hold on to the moment a little while longer.

No one had ever made her feel so good. So right. And this man was a total novice. A smile curved her lips. Well, he wasn't a novice any more. If he had ever really been one.

And neither was she.

He groaned and lifted off her, rolling—or rather flopping—onto his back beside her.

They were both staring at the ceiling now.

She turned her head, to find him watching her intently.

'What is your name?' he asked, his tone gruff.

She chuckled. She couldn't help it.

That had to be the afterglow talking, surely?

Totally.

'Cara. Cara Moira Doyle. I'm named after my maternal grandmother, who was by all accounts a fierce woman. I wish I had met her. Sorry, that's probably TMI again.'

Okay, Cara, stop talking before you exhaust the poor man.

She pursed her lips, but she couldn't prevent her smile spreading at the thought that he already seemed a little shattered, and she was the cause.

'Hello, Cara,' he said, and emotion tightened around her ribs.

'Hello, Logan, it's been a pleasure,' she said as another laugh bubbled out of her mouth.

For goodness' sake, stop giggling like a moonstruck girl.

But even as she tried to control the smile on her lips, it refused to leave her heart. She knew this was just sex—even if it was really spectacular sex—but the truth was, she felt impossibly grateful to him, for showing her that there had never been anything wrong with her. That the men—no, the boys—she'd kissed before, and Barry O'Connell in particular, who had treated her with so little care or affection or tenderness, then told her she was frigid when she had asked him to stop, had been as much to blame for her appalling experience of sex as she was.

She was twenty-one years old and she'd been avoiding sex ever since the night of her Debs—which would be appalling, if it weren't so pathetic.

Her first lover was staring at her now as if she were the most curiously puzzling thing he had ever seen. And strangely she liked it. Who said Cara Doyle couldn't be a femme fatale?

'What is this TMI?' he asked.

She choked out another laugh.

Ah, well, so much for being a femme fatale.

'It just stands for "too much information". I have a tendency to talk a lot when I'm nervous.'

'Why are you nervous?' he asked, a frown puckering his forehead.

'Because, well…' How to answer such a direct question without making it seem as if what they had just done had meant far too much to her? Far more than it should?

It was her turn to frown.

'Because I guess I don't know you… And we've just done something I thought I'd never do, and certainly never enjoy. And I enjoyed that a lot.'

She clamped her mouth shut, but the flush fired across her collarbone regardless.

'For me too,' he said easily as his gaze dropped to her breasts.

She folded her arms across the yearning flesh, before he could notice her nipples hardening again, the memory of how he had played with them so enthusiastically making the endorphins ramp right back up to eleven.

'I'm glad,' she managed, suddenly feeling exposed. 'Although that's not saying much, seeing as I'm the first woman you've ever had sex with.'

His gaze rose back to her face, that patient, probing stare as intimidating as it was exciting. 'And I am your first too.'

Ah, yes, you did let that slip in the heat of the moment. Strike one to Cara Doyle's big mouth.

'Well, yes,' she said as her blush incinerated her cheeks.

'We have a powerful sexual connection,' he murmured.

She stared at him, not sure what to say, having lost the power of speech. Had she ever met a man more forthright? She didn't think so. And why did it make her a little sad to think that was all he felt they shared?

'It would certainly seem so,' she said at last.

He lifted up on his elbow to lean over her, then ran his thumb down the side of her face, before hooking her unruly hair behind her ear. The casual, but surprisingly tender caress made her whole body shudder. A fierce emotion flashed into those pale blue eyes, as his gaze roamed over her face—gauging her reaction. But before she could read his expression, the emotion was banked again behind that intense stare. 'It is a shame we cannot explore it more,' he said, as much to himself as her.

'Why can't we?' she asked, then wanted to kick herself when his eyebrows rose.

Strike two to Cara Doyle's big mouth.

'Because you must leave,' he said.

But she could hear what he hadn't said.

Because I do not want you here.

She grabbed the sheet from the end of the bed and yanked it up to cover herself as she sat up. He was still lounging beside her, completely comfortable in his nakedness. Her gaze snagged on the evidence that he still wanted her, but clearly not enough.

'Yes, right,' she said, then cringed at the disappointment in her voice.

Seriously, Cara, could you sound any more needy? And desperate?

'No, it's grand,' she said hastily. 'You're right. I need to get back to Saariselkä and upload my photos. If my camera hasn't been destroyed by the cold.'

She shut her mouth, aware she was starting to babble again. Time to make a hasty retreat. And regroup. Her body was still flushed, and that semi-erection he was sporting was making her want to do foolish things again... With him.

But he no longer wanted to do them with her.

So what if he'd rocked her world—*twice*—and made her feel special? It was all simply an illusion. Because he'd made it perfectly clear he wanted her gone now.

She tried to stifle the foolish feeling of rejection. What had she expected? She'd made it clear this wasn't a big deal—her virginity and his an inconvenience brought about by circumstance. That it had taken her this long to get over the stigma of her father's abuse, and the likes of Barry O'Connell's cruel taunts and teenage ineptitude, wasn't anything to do with him.

Plus, she *did* need to return to Saariselkä as soon as possible. She had her career to think about. Her new-found endorphins would just have to get over themselves.

She shifted off the bed, dragging the sheet with her, attempting to keep all the essential bits covered so she could make a swift and dignified exit. But as she stood, he leaned across the bed and grasped her wrist. The sheet slipped.

'You are upset,' he said as she grappled to cover herself and her dignity. 'Why?'

She stiffened, hating herself for the surge of emotion that felt stupidly like gratitude. Because he had noticed. And asked.

She tugged her arm free of his grasp, feeling exposed now and ashamed of how needy she was for any sign of affection from him. The afterglow had faded—and what had made her feel powerful, even cherished, during their epic sex session, now made her feel pathetic.

Cara, you eejit. Why did you throw yourself at him?

She swallowed past the shame threatening to close her throat, and reminding her far too forcefully of her teenage years, growing up with a man who had called her a slut more than once when she was still no more than a girl.

'I'm fine,' she lied.

But as she galvanised herself to walk away, he leapt off the bed and grasped her arm again.

'This is not the truth,' he said, although he dropped her arm as soon as she struggled.

'I'm *not* upset,' she said, as she rubbed her wrist where his touch still burned.

If her thigh muscles were still trembling, and her nipples as hard as torpedoes ready to launch, that was neither here nor there. Her body had a mind of its own where he was concerned, that much was obvious, but why was she letting her emotions become involved? He had offered her nothing. But nor did she want anything more from him.

He frowned. 'You cannot stay…' he said.

'And I didn't ask to, fella,' she huffed, furious now that he could see through her show of bravado so easily. Enough to know that she yearned for something more, some sign of intimacy, that went way beyond the physical.

What was that even about?

She bit into her lip and stared down at her hands, which had white-knuckled on the sheet, as she tried to control the brutal blush.

He raked his fingers through his hair, looking frustrated, then strode across the room to his dresser. Tugging out a fresh pair of boxer shorts, he put them on, but they didn't do much to hide the effect she still had on him.

She should walk out. Why was she still standing here like an eejit, waiting for something she shouldn't even need? Or want.

But she couldn't seem to detach her gaze from his.

He was watching her with that intense concentration that turned her thigh muscles to mush and made the lump swell in her throat.

What was he thinking? And why did he have to look so gorgeous when he had treated her as if she were a…? She pushed the ugly word back down her throat.

That was her da talking.

Perhaps she was oversensitive about other people's opinions of her virtue, because of all the names that man had called her, when she'd barely understood what they meant. And why should she care anyway what Logan Colton thought of her? His opinion didn't matter—any more than her da's had.

But still, she couldn't seem to get her feet to move.

At last, his gaze detached from her face and glanced out of the huge windows.

Night had already fallen, and she could see snow swirling again in the frozen air outside the glass, depressing her even more. What if the storm kicked off again, and she had to stay another night?

How could she bear the humiliation? The knowing that somehow, somewhere, in some foolish corner of her heart, she had hoped for more from him? Had needed more?

'We will leave at first light tomorrow,' he said. 'Once you are returned to your vehicle, you can call for rescue.'

She nodded, but there was something in his voice—something wary and defensive—that didn't make any sense.

'Good,' she said, even as that foolish feeling of disappointment pushed at her chest.

She grabbed her discarded clothing and finally made her exit from his bedroom. But as she returned to her room, took a long hot shower, and found herself attempting to scrub off the scent of sex that clung to her skin, her father's angry words echoed in her head.

The brutal shame engulfed her again, because those words still had the power to hurt and humiliate her—after all this time.

But as she lay in bed afterwards, she thought of Logan, wild and untamed—and the intense silvery blue gaze that hid so many secrets. He had made love to her with such passion and purpose—she'd been the centre of his universe and she'd loved it. And then the memory of her father's words had turned the whole experience to crap.

But she could also recall the flash of regret in Logan's eyes as he had informed her he would take her to her snowmobile first thing in the morning. And suddenly, nothing seemed clear any more.

She had taken offence at his desire to be rid of her, because some of that abused girl still lurked inside her—needing validation and approval from a man.

Thanks, Da.

But what if his insistence that she had to leave had never been about her? Had always been about his fierce need for privacy, for solitude, his desperation to shun human contact?

She had breached his defences, but because of her own insecurities, she hadn't pushed her advantage.

She rolled over on the bed, curled into herself. And wanted to scream. Finally forced to admit the truth... She didn't want to leave first thing tomorrow.

He fascinated her and excited her in a way no other man ever had. Plus, she'd waited this long to finally know what all the fuss was about sex, and it had been glorious.

How did she let all that go, without any regrets?

But how did she ask him to let her stay, without seeming needy and pathetic? And how did she get him to admit he wanted to explore that connection too, without exposing herself and her emotions even more?

Damn the man!

CHAPTER SEVEN

LOGAN BRAKED HIS snowmobile as they entered the forest clearing where Cara's broken vehicle lay buried under a drift. Cara's arms loosened from around his waist. And let go.

His breath eased out through lungs tight with something he couldn't name… Something he did not want to name.

He'd spent the long winter night working furiously on his latest piece. Tempering the block of solid pine to carve it into the basic form of a golden eagle in flight. And trying not to think about the woman in his home. And the moment when he had come apart inside her.

But of course, it had been impossible.

He never should have touched her. He should have known it would make him lose focus. Force him into a situation he didn't understand.

He still hadn't figured out what they had argued about afterwards, but then his mind had been shattered, so no surprise there.

But as she climbed off his snowmobile and headed across the clearing towards her buried vehicle, his gaze remained fixed on her. She was dressed in six layers of thermal clothing, so it was hard to make out her shape, but the padded disguise did nothing to stop the memory of her skin—soft, malleable, responsive beneath his fingertips, his tongue—blasting into his brain.

He ripped off his goggles.

Aware that he was becoming aroused… Again.

This was an addiction, already. One single taste of her had turned him into a sex addict. Not good. When he had to let her go now.

They had barely spoken when she had appeared in the kitchen this morning. She had looked as if she hadn't slept well at all. He would have taken some comfort from that, except he had hardly slept himself.

He dismounted to follow her across the clearing.

He stood and watched as she dug through the snow with her gloved hands—frantic to get to the camera equipment he had left out here.

At last, she found the saddlebag. But the three pairs of gloves she had on made it impossible for her to open the bag and remove the camera equipment.

She pulled down her balaclava, to expose her mouth. Those full lips that had been wrapped around his…

He closed his eyes, trying to expel the memories, far too aware of the heat pooling in his groin.

'Can you help me get this undone?' she shouted.

Forcing himself to remember his plan—to check the camera and make sure she had not taken any pictures that might identify the location of his home—he took it from her. But after opening the bag and hand-ing the camera back to her, he watched as she tried to get the equipment to start.

Five minutes later, they were forced to give up.

'It is too cold,' he said, aware that he would be forced to trust her, if he left her here without checking what was on it. 'Better to try and start it once it is warm.'

She nodded. 'How far is it to Saariselkä?'

'I cannot take you there,' he said, the old panic rising up his throat.

He could not step foot in the thriving tourist resort. It was too much to ask of him.

She seemed surprised, but then indicated the busted snowmobile. 'Can you help me to get this working?' she asked.

'I am not a mechanic,' he replied—which was not entirely true. He had learned how to service and maintain all the vehicles he kept on his property, including two motorised sledges and a snowmobile. He could usually fix most mechanical problems, so he would not have to seek outside help. It was one of the basic requirements of being self-sufficient in such a harsh environment. But, repairing the machine in this location, when the thermometer was scheduled to dip below minus twenty today, would be difficult, if not impossible.

Plus, he'd checked the machine two days ago, when he'd found her camera. It was a wreck. Who knew what she had paid for it? But she had taken her life into her hands riding it so far out into the wilderness.

His suspicions about her motives returned.

How could he let her go now, when he hadn't been able to check the pictures on the camera? Surely he had every right to insist she return with him now to his home? Just to be sure.

But even as he tried to persuade himself his desire to ask her to come back was all about preserving the privacy he had maintained for so long, he knew that wasn't the whole truth. Not even close. Because he could still recall the look of disappointment, even sadness, in her eyes last night, after they had made love.

A look that had triggered the yearning he had been trying to ignore all through the night.

The truth was, he wished to make love to her again... And again. To explore the longing, until it had run its course and he could return to the peace he had known before he had met her.

But what scared him more was the knowledge that his urge to keep her wasn't just about the livewire physical connection that was even now pulsing in his groin.

He had lain awake last night until the early hours of the morning, long before dawn, after working himself into a virtual coma in his workshop and then in the gym, thinking about that look, and the words she had said.

'Why can't we...?'

And the words she hadn't.

Explore it more.

Even though the request had made no sense, she had put the thought into his head. And now he could not dispel it. He had re-examined the tone and texture of her voice, recalled in exquisite detail the different tendrils of her scent as she stood so proud and belligerent in his bedroom, with that sheet barely covering her...

Until he'd finally fallen into a fitful sleep only a few hours before the sunrise.

When she had appeared in the kitchen, he had been struck all over again by the rush of adrenaline—the desperate yearning—that hadn't gone away during the night.

The woman was a sorceress. Letting her stay would threaten everything that had made him whole for so long. But still the thought could do nothing to dispel the insistent desire not to let her go. Not yet.

'So what do we do now?' she asked.

We? Why had she said we? When they were not friends. And they never could be. He had never relied on anyone, not since his grandfather's death when he was a boy of nineteen.

He shook his head, trying to dislodge the confusing thoughts. And make himself concentrate on what had to happen now.

The plan had always been to leave her here, after checking her camera, while she waited for rescue. But after last night, he couldn't seem to commit to all the reasons why he had to stick to his plan.

'Don't trust anyone, Arto, they are all just vultures who want to hurt you the way they hurt your mother...'

His grandfather's oft-repeated warnings echoed in his head—but could do nothing to quell the insistent desire that continued to spike in his gut and make him want things he shouldn't need.

And an answer he didn't recognise spilled out of his mouth.

'I could arrange to have the vehicle towed and repaired. You can stay with me until it is ready?'

The reckless offer shocked him—but not as much as the strange yearning that assailed him as he waited for her reply. Or the brutal rush of relief when her face softened.

'I'd… I'd like that. If you're sure it's not too much trouble.'

It *was* too much trouble. She was a threat. Someone he would be a fool to trust.

But even so, he couldn't find the will to do anything but nod.

She remained silent as he called his contact in the local Saami community on his satellite phone and gave the older man the location of the broken snowmobile. He had always trusted the old friend of his grandfather's not to give away his whereabouts—but this was the first time he had asked for his assistance in ten years.

As he threw his leg over his machine, his breath blooming in the frozen air—he couldn't shake the thought that he had exposed himself.

But as he settled in the seat and switched on the ignition, he forced himself not to second-guess himself again. He couldn't withdraw the offer now. Nor did he want to. But surely this yearning, this need was about nothing more than the intense sexual connection they had discovered last night.

Of course, he would want to explore it. Why wouldn't he? Especially as she had made it clear she wished to explore it too. That did not mean he needed to trust her with anything else.

She climbed up behind him, then pressed herself against his back. Even through all the layers of clothing, he could imagine her subtle curves moulding to the hard line of his back. His heart stuttered as her arms wrapped around his midriff again and held him tight.

He manoeuvred the vehicle in a circle, to back it out of the clearing, then shot off along the tracks they'd made in the snow, to return to his sanctuary.

But this time, he was forced to acknowledge, he had invited her into his home… Willingly.

His heart hammered against his chest wall.

He did not know what that heavy beat was even about.

Until he convinced himself it was simply the bone-deep longing to have her again. In any way she would let him.

As they traversed the icy terrain, the adrenaline surged.

Why was he making this so complicated? And why was he second-guessing every decision? What possible threat could she really represent? The only reason he wanted, or needed, her company was to satisfy this vicious desire. This endless yearning. But once that was fed, once he had gorged on her, and she him, they would tire of each other. Solitude had always been his strength, and no woman could ever change that. Not even one as beautiful and confusing and fascinating as this one.

Cara felt the snowmobile's engine rumble through her over-eager body as she clung to Logan, her face buried into his back to escape from the wind.

She was tired, exhausted even, from a virtually sleepless night spent going over and over in her brain what she should do next.

But she could hardly deny the feeling of regret as they'd driven out into the wintry landscape this morning, or the shattered relief when he had suggested returning to his house. Together.

She didn't want to leave yet. Which was madness, she understood that. But at least she had her camera equipment now. So, she hadn't completely jettisoned her professional priorities in favour of her newly discovered libido.

Logan had been brusque and businesslike when she'd appeared this morning, waiting for her to have a quick breakfast then get dressed in the cumbersome thermal clothing before meeting him in the garage.

The forest thickened and then opened out onto the huge frozen lake system that surrounded Logan's home. The sun was high in the sky now, the eerie blue light making the snowy wilderness twinkle and glow. Her nose and eyelashes had begun to freeze even under her goggles, her extremities losing feeling even as he shielded her from the wind. She could feel his warmth through the snowsuit, his strength as he handled the cumbersome machine with consummate skill.

How could she have slept with him last night and still not know him at all? Had she made a mistake accepting his offer so eagerly? Especially as he still hadn't mentioned last night. Why hadn't she demanded to know exactly what his offer entailed?

She huffed, trying to slice off all the unhelpful thoughts before they could take root.

At last, the stunning glass and steel structure appeared on the horizon.

She frowned as her heart rate spiked.

As he arrived at the lakeside entrance to the house, and clicked the gizmo attached to the snowmobile, the garage door rose. He drove into the concrete bunker, the warm air like a welcome blanket as the door lowered behind them.

But inside Cara felt cold—and foolish. She'd jumped at the chance to return here—because he still fascinated and excited her. But why hadn't she made more of an effort to find out where they stood?

As soon as he braked, Cara clambered off the machine. She ripped off her head coverings, and tugged off her snowsuit, then took off her ski jacket and fleece while he parked the vehicle.

She reached for the camera box she had tucked into his saddlebag while he took off the first layers of his own clothing.

He slicked back his hair, damp from sweat, the day-old growth on his jaw making him look like a pirate as he walked towards her.

He reached for her camera. 'Let me see it,' he demanded.

She held the camera close to her chest and shook her head. 'Why?' she asked, hoping against hope that her suspicions were wrong.

But the cold feeling spread as she waited for his reply. Because she suspected she already knew the answer to that question. Despite the offer to bring her back here, he still didn't trust her.

He tucked his hands into the pockets of his ski-pants and levelled that all-seeing glare at her, the one designed to intimidate her into not asking inconvenient or probing questions.

Well, to heck with that.

He'd been inside her. He'd been her first lover. And maybe that didn't make her any more trustworthy in his eyes. But it meant something to her.

Rather a lot in fact.

She didn't trust men easily, but on some elemental level she had trusted him. Enough to throw herself at him. Enough to want to come back here at his suggestion. But she would be damned if she'd do that entirely on his terms. He wanted her camera now, so he could check what was on it. She got that. And she didn't really have any objection to that. Because she knew her pictures would confirm her innocence.

But she would be damned if she would let him believe he had a right to make her prove her innocence, when she had done nothing wrong—except get lost in the snowy wilderness, and want him, the way he wanted her.

He continued to stare at her, and for once she could see the calculation in his eyes. He was trying to decide whether to admit the truth or not.

She was sure he was going to give her some lame excuse, but then he surprised her.

'Because I want to see if you took any pictures of my home before you became lost,' he said. 'No one is allowed to know this exact location unless they have signed NDAs and I know I can trust them.'

'But what about the people who built this place?' she blurted out, a little stunned even now by the extent of his seclusion, and how fiercely he protected it.

'The construction crews, the architect and engineer were all blindfolded before they were driven here. And also required to sign NDAs.'

'But… How do you get your food delivered? What about if you need a doctor?'

'I have supplies air-dropped to a location twenty miles away twice a month. I can contact a doctor in an emergency. But I am fit and healthy.'

'But… *Why?*' She could see instantly the question had angered him, his eyes becoming flat and direct, the muscle twitching in his jaw visible despite the heavy beard scruff.

'Because I value my privacy,' he said.

He'd got away with the non-answer once before, but she refused to let him get away with it again.

'But why do you value it to that extent? What are you afraid of?'

The muscle hardened, his brows furrowing over those piercing silvery blue eyes.

'I am not afraid. I just do not need people.'

It seemed like a simple answer, but the stormy emotions on his face told a very different story.

Something had happened, something *must* have happened to make him so wary of social contact, so determined never to be found.

Sympathy pulsed in her chest.

'How long have you lived out here alone?' she asked.

'Since my grandfather died a decade ago. He brought me here to save me from the vultures after my parents' death. And I have no desire to return to that circus.'

The vultures? Was he talking about the press? All she knew about him was the things she could vaguely recall her bar colleague mentioning—that he had disappeared from the public eye as a child.

Oh, for an Internet connection, or a phone signal, or a charger for her phone. There wasn't much she wouldn't do right now to be able to do an Internet search on him.

But somehow, she doubted she would find much. And why should she need to do an Internet search, when she had him right in front of her?

She decided to push her luck. 'How old were you when your parents died?'

His gaze narrowed, suspicion rife in his eyes. 'Ten.'

The sympathy contracted around her ribs like a vice.

He had come to Finland while still an impression-
able child, after what had to have been a traumatic
event, and then had been left in the care of a man who
had clearly kept him isolated from the world. Was it
any surprise he was a recluse?

'How did your parents die, Logan?'

He flinched, as if she had slapped him, and she saw
the pain flash across his features.

'You don't know?' he asked, the sceptical tone only
wounding her more.

She shook her head.

He glanced past her, his stance tense, his eyes closing briefly. She sensed the struggle he waged. This
was not something he wished to remember, let alone
talk about.

What right did she really have to ask him about
any of this? They'd slept together once. But just as
she said, 'It's okay, you don't have to answer—' He
interrupted her.

'They were shot. A kidnap attempt gone wrong.'

'Someone was trying to kidnap them?' she asked,
shocked to her core.

'Not them, *me*,' he murmured. But that rigid tone
broke on the last word.

Had he been there? He must have been. Which
meant he must have witnessed their deaths. The
thought horrified her and made the sympathy tangle
into a knot in her belly.

Before she could think better of the impulse, she
stepped forward, and pressed her palm to his cheek.

The muscle flexed and hardened, but she could see the brittle anguish in his gaze before he could mask it.

'I'm so sorry, Logan…'

He clasped her wrist, dragged her hand away from his face, the pain in his eyes turning to heat, and hunger. 'No more questions,' he said.

She nodded. 'No, no more questions.'

'I want you still,' he said, the brutal honesty, the need he couldn't hide, making the knot of sympathy turn into something fierce and visceral and undeniable. 'Show me what's on the camera,' he demanded.

A part of her wanted to refuse the request. But she understood now, he had answered her questions to earn her trust. How could she refuse to do the same? She pulled the strap off her shoulder and handed him the camera.

He took the Leica and switched it on. For several seconds that felt like years, the mechanism whirled as the camera's batteries warmed. Anticipation and hope clogged her throat. And fear. What if the camera still wouldn't start?

She swallowed heavily. Determined not to examine the fact that her desire to rescue her photos was all wrapped up in the desire to prove to him he could trust her too.

At last, the viewfinder lit. Relief guttered through her as he clicked methodically through the photos she'd taken.

He came to the end of the memory card. His gaze connected with hers as he turned the camera off.

'They are good,' he said.

Pride swelled in her chest. She banked it, ruthlessly. His opinion of her work shouldn't matter. She reached for the camera, but he held it away from her.

'You will not need it, while you are here,' he said.

She pushed her anger to the fore, to cover the well of disappointment. Apparently, she still hadn't earned his trust.

'I promise not to take pictures of you, or your home,' she offered, tightly. '*If* I decide to stay,' she clarified. Because he seemed to assume that was already a foregone conclusion.

Whatever happened now, whatever she agreed to, she refused to be treated like a stranger, or a threat— to be trusted even less than the people he had forced to sign NDAs.

'But it's my camera,' she continued. 'And if you can't trust me to have possession of it while I'm here, then I *can't* stay here… I won't.'

His brows flattened, his lips tightening. And the muscle she'd noticed several times before in his cheek began to twitch.

He did not like the idea of letting her have the camera. But she refused to back down. His gaze roamed over her face, gauging her determination.

The seconds ticked by as her ribs contracted, and the pounding in her ears became deafening.

But finally, he lowered the precious Leica and offered it to her. She took it hastily, determined not to examine the thundering rush of relief that flowed through her.

The concession felt huge though. Especially when he said, 'While you are here… I want you in my bed.'

It didn't really sound like a question, more of a demand. So what else was new? But he had at least finally acknowledged what he was really offering her.

And given her the opening she needed.

'Okay, but I have some ground rules,' she managed, not even sure what they were yet, but determined not to appear like some witless fool, completely captivated by his potent sex appeal… Even if she was.

Because, after all, the melting sensation in her core didn't lie as she sucked in a lungful of his delicious scent and sensation pulsed across her lips as his gaze centred on her mouth.

'Rules?' he said, the curve in those firm sensual lips even more captivating than the dark awareness she recognised in his gaze. She had no idea what was so amusing. 'What rules?'

She cleared her throat. 'I-important rules,' she managed.

'Uh-huh…'

The rumble of his reply streaked through her as he stepped closer. Close enough to touch. Close enough to have her body readying itself for him.

The storm of sensation threatened to derail her again. But she found the strength to plant her palms against his chest. The hard pectoral muscles flexed as she edged him back.

'A week, I can't stay more than a week,' she said. 'If the skimobile isn't fixed by then, you'll have to take me back to Saariselkä,' she managed.

'Two weeks,' he countered. 'A week will not be long enough.'

The fierce need in his eyes made her insides turn to mush. Had any man ever looked at her like that before, as if he could not get enough of her?

No, never.

'T-ten days,' she said, even though she had the strange thought she was arguing against herself now, as well as him. 'And I get to keep working, during daylight hours.' She could build her portfolio here as well as anywhere—so her time wouldn't be wasted.

Plus, it was the principle of the thing... Wasn't it?

He hooked a finger into the waistband of her sweatpants and tugged her back towards him. She dragged in a lungful of his scent—that intoxicating mix of bergamot and pine that drove her wild.

'Two weeks,' he demanded again. 'In my bed. And you may take photos away from the house, as long as I am with you.'

Then he took the camera off her shoulder, placed it on the ground.

'Say yes, Cara,' he urged, his voice gruff with demand. 'Two weeks and then I will ensure you get back to Saariselkä.'

How could she resist him, when every cell in her body was begging her to give in?

And maybe this was what she needed, to finally become herself at last, a woman in every sense of the word, no longer bound by the shame of that little girl.

'Okay,' she managed, her throat dry, her panties already soaking wet.

He let out a triumphant huff, then scooped her into his arms and strode out of the garage.

Two weeks.

She'd agreed to two weeks, she thought vaguely as she let him carry her back through his home to his bedroom. Like a trophy. A prize.

But as they stripped each other, and he sank back into her at last, his thick erection stretched her tender flesh as an orgasm barrelled towards her.

She'd taken a risk. And this was her reward. They had an understanding now. Maybe he still didn't trust her completely, but he trusted her enough.

She let herself shatter and held him as he crashed over into the abyss behind her.

Hadn't she earned this? she thought vaguely. After nearly killing herself to make her career a reality? Didn't she deserve the chance to be reckless and impulsive for once? And unafraid?

But as she sank into an exhausted sleep, her heart thundering as his big body wrapped around her, she made herself a solemn promise.

Take the risk. Just don't you dare risk your heart in the process, Cara.

CHAPTER EIGHT

'WAKE UP, CARA...you are getting lazy.'

'Huh?' Cara huffed and opened eyes heavy with sleep to find Logan leaning over her, with a disturbingly gorgeous smile on his face. This was new—he usually looked so focussed and intense. Her heart bounced in her chest.

'I'm not lazy. I'm shattered,' she murmured, her voice rough as she struggled to wake from the sex-induced coma he'd put her in last night. Sunlight sparkled through the floor-to-ceiling windows in his bedroom. How long had she been out? It had been pitch-dark when she'd finally plunged into a dreamless sleep.

The man was insatiable.

'*You* shattered me. Now get lost,' she grumbled, presenting her back to him as she rolled over and pulled the duvet over her head.

How on earth did he have the energy to get out of bed? Let alone look at her with that hot awareness in his eyes.

They'd made love too many times to count in the

past week, in the seven energetic days and long sultry nights since they'd made their Devil's Bargain. They'd christened pretty much every room in the house, even the gym and his workshop, and then there had been that memorable moment yesterday afternoon in the kitchen—when he'd bent her over the work surface while she was slicing carrots, worked her into a frenzy with his tongue and then plunged into her from behind. She was lucky she hadn't lost a finger in the process.

Heat flushed through her tired—and frankly sore—body as she burrowed into the bedding.

The man was a sex machine. Inventive, inquisitive, generous and curious. And it seemed he had stored up a ton of fantasies over his long years of celibacy to practise on her. And while she had enjoyed every second of his attention—each orgasm more overpowering and overwhelming than the last as he discovered every possible way he could arouse and entice her—she was not in the market for any more orgasms until she had slept for at least twenty-four hours straight. Especially as in the last few days that disturbing sense of anxiety was never far behind.

She yelped as he flipped the duvet off her bare body.

'Up,' he said in that take-no-prisoners tone she had come to adore—and hate—in equal measure. 'We are wasting daylight.'

'Go. Away!' she shouted as she grappled with the duvet.

'No,' he said, before he won the duvet war and whisked it off the bed.

The arousal in his eyes darkened with intent as his gaze roamed over her yearning flesh. The answering heat in her belly flared. Because of course it did!

She knew what that look meant. And she had discovered she was powerless to resist it. But if she had any more orgasms, she might actually die.

'We are not having sex!' she announced, determined to persuade her traitorous body as much as him, because seriously, how could she be wet for him again? When she was still a little sore from their last epic session.

Clearly Logan Colton was not the only sex addict in this room. Because the hot brick that had been jammed between her legs for seven days had already begun to pulse again.

'Understood,' he said, surprising her—because the man had to be able to smell her arousal. And she knew by now he usually pressed that advantage every chance he got.

But before she could evade him, or congratulate herself on sticking to her guns, he scooped her off the bed and hefted her onto his shoulder.

The air expelled from her lungs, and it took her a moment to find her outrage, through the shock.

'Logan, what the hell?' she yelped, holding on to the chuckle that threatened to burst out of her mouth.

If she laughed at his outrageous behaviour she'd be lost, because surely he would take that as an invitation… Because he took *everything* as an invitation.

She struggled, desperately trying to ignore the flutter of excitement and affection making her lungs hurt and the hot brick in her belly weightless. He was usually so serious about sex, his concentration whenever he caressed her his own special superpower—because it made him impossible to resist. Playfulness was a new look for him. The problem was, it only made him more irresistible.

She pressed her palms into the solid muscles of his back, trying to lift herself, twisting and turning and ignoring the swooping sensation in her belly that threatened to beckon emotions she'd kept so carefully in check for over a week.

Before she could get too sentimental though, his large hand landed firmly on her backside.

'Stop squirming or I will drop you,' he said.

'Then put me down, you *dolt*,' she yelped and struggled harder.

But as he headed through the house, apparently oblivious to her protests, and the fact that they were both stark nekkid, the laughter escaped.

When he finally deposited her in the garage—beside a pile of neatly folded clothing he must have washed for her while she slept—her heart bobbed into her throat, the wicked glint in those pale blue eyes turning them into a magnetic silver.

'Dress before you freeze,' he ordered as that stark possessive gaze raked over her burning flesh again. 'Or I decide to make you beg me for another orgasm.'

'I don't beg, fella,' she scoffed.

But she darted away from him before he decided to test that theory. After all, they both knew she was putty in his hands—whatever her best intentions.

As she scrambled into the layers of clothing, she watched him dress himself in a more leisurely fashion, immune to the lower ambient temperature in the garage, and tried not to regret not taking him up on his offer of yet more orgasms.

Because sex was safer than seeing this new, almost boyish side to the harsh, demanding man she had spent the last week with. A side he'd never let her see before now. A side she hadn't even known existed.

Not a big deal, Cara. In two weeks you'd have to find something else to do eventually.

'So where exactly are we going?' she asked as she stamped on her boots and zipped up the cumbersome snowsuit, feeling surprisingly enthusiastic about this new adventure. Perhaps she wasn't that tired after all. And getting out of the house had to be a good thing.

They hadn't left his Fortress of Solitude—now renamed the Fortress of Sex-capades—since last weekend, when they'd originally agreed to indulge their 'sexual connection'. The only times they'd been apart was while he worked in his workshop and she worked up a sweat in the gym. She hadn't even been able to venture out to check out the local wildlife because the weather had been terrible.

With the sun shining today for the first time in a week, it was way past time they found some new ways to amuse themselves. Because she was starting to get beard burn in places where it had no right to be. And that damn anxious feeling was starting to concern her.

Logan finished shrugging on his own layers, then walked to her. He zipped up her suit the rest of the way, then helped her to put on her outer gloves and the different face coverings that would protect her cheeks from the frosty air. Her heart pummelled her chest wall, her ribs feeling suspiciously tight at the methodical way he checked her clothing, to ensure she was appropriately attired. He lifted her chin, that mocking smile making her heart rate slow dangerously.

How could he look even more gorgeous when he was annoying the heck out of her?

'I am going to introduce you to the benefits of ice swimming,' he announced.

'Wait? *What?*' she asked, sure she hadn't heard that correctly. 'You're not serious?'

'It will revive you,' he said, that playful smile taking a wicked turn.

'No, it won't. It'll kill me,' she managed. Before she could object further, though, he had hefted her back onto his shoulder and ordered the garage door open in Finnish.

As the icy air hit her cheeks, her renewed protests—as he trudged out into the snow and headed towards the frozen lake—turned out to be completely futile. Because her cries of outrage were muffled by the three balaclavas covering her mouth. And her flailing arms and feet were bundled up in seven layers of Arctic clothing, insulating his broad back from the fallout.

The rat.

'I will go in first. You must descend quickly or your fingers will freeze to the ladder,' Logan commanded, unable to take his eyes off Cara as they stood on the edge of the swimming hole. She wore nothing but a pair of his boxer shorts, sliders to protect her feet and the thick robe he'd given her, which reached her ankles. With her arms folded tightly across her chest he could see the delicious hint of cleavage flushed pink from the sauna.

It had been an act of sheer willpower not to take advantage of all that lush skin as they had heated themselves to prepare for their swim. She hadn't commented on the erection stretching his shorts. But he could tell from the potent scent of her arousal she had noticed it.

But then, he was almost permanently ready for her, in a constant state of wanting to touch, to taste, to devour.

In the past week he had lost the last of his inhibitions, the fear that he might hurt her. And taken her whenever and wherever he could.

She had embraced the sex with the same enthusiasm, the same fierce, unquenchable desire—meeting all of his demands and making many of her own. And he had discovered a level of pleasure, of passion, he had never believed possible.

As he had watched her sleep this morning, her slender body laid out on his bed like a banquet, the heat had pooled in his crotch all over again, but he had forced himself not to wake her—and demand more. Because as he had studied her, he had finally noticed the ravages of the past week's endless sex-capades, as Cara had dubbed them, on her soft skin.

The small thumb-sized bruises on her hips where he had held her too tightly, the slight rash around both nipples where he had sucked her into a frenzy too many times to count—because she was so deliciously sensitive there. He had listened to the deep murmur of her breathing, a sign of her exhaustion, and been more than a little ashamed.

How could he have gorged on her again and again, and still not have satisfied this endless hunger? Was this normal? This desperate clawing need to touch and caress and excite? And to be touched and caressed and excited in return? After so many years spent avoiding any touch at all?

And when was it going to stop? Would this thirst ever be fully quenched? Because they only had seven days left and already he was terrified she had changed him in some fundamental way.

As much as he had tried to make their connection only about the physical, there were so many other aspects of her presence in his home that had begun to enchant him.

The inane chatter about nothing in particular, which had become a comforting background noise when they cooked and ate together. The flush that highlighted the freckles on her cleavage when he frustrated or aroused her. The way she whistled off-key, songs by an Irish band called U2, when she stirred the big pots of stew they had been devouring each evening before devouring each other.

Instead of enjoying his solitude, he now sought her company.

Instead of wanting to know nothing more about her than how to make her beg for release, he wanted to know everything. Who she was? Where did she come from? Who were the brothers she had mentioned in passing with such affection? Why had she waited so long to have sex when she was so responsive to a man's touch? What did that band's songs really sound like when she wasn't mangling them? What had driven her to come to Finnish Lapland and take the stunning shots he had seen on her camera?

He had even had to catch himself from offering to take her outside in a blizzard when he had found her studying a snowy owl as it swooped past the bedroom windows.

The woman was an artist, just as he was. He had seen her fierce desire to capture the bird in flight and understood it. So much so, that he was even beginning to feel uncomfortable about making her keep her promise not to use the camera around his home.

How had he come to be desperate to know everything about her? How could he want to please her, and not just her body? Because both were urges he did not understand.

He had never been curious about another human being. Never wanted to please anyone but himself. Not since he was a boy and he had first arrived in the care of his grandfather—and this frozen wilderness had become his sanctuary. A place of peace and solitude.

But his sanctuary didn't feel as safe and sure as it once had—when he imagined it now without her in it.

'I can't believe I'm actually doing this. It's madness!' she huffed, stamping her feet, her breath pluming out in a cloud.

He grinned at her disgruntled expression and shoved the wayward thoughts to the back of his mind.

Time to stop thinking and start doing.

They both needed time out from the unquenchable desire, and he couldn't think of a better way to control it than dousing himself in icy water. That he had wanted to share this with her too was problematic, but he had been unable to deny the urge.

He dropped his own robe, slung it over the ladder and climbed into the water.

The prickling pain fired over his skin as he immersed himself, his panting breaths helping to regulate his temperature.

'Come quickly, before you cool too much.' He beckoned her in.

A delightful frown puckered her brow, and she muttered something that sounded like, 'Oh, feck it.' Then, with the fierceness he had come to adore, she slipped the robe off, revealing those pert breasts, and flipped off her sliders.

Turning, she presented him with a perfect view of her beautiful butt, exquisitely displayed in his shorts. He kicked away from the ladder, giving her space as her toe touched the water.

She swore profusely, the profane words echoing off the quiet snow and making birds fly up from the nearby trees. He began to laugh, as he watched her scrambling down into the frigid lake. She ducked in all the way to her neckline, panting furiously and still cursing like a sailor.

'Good?' he asked, as he swam closer—the endorphin rush starting to shoot into his brain, making his whole body sing.

'F-f-freezing!' she shouted over her shoulder, then clambered back up the ladder again so fast her bright pink skin was a blur of motion. Her breasts jiggled adorably as she danced around trying to grab her robe, her nipples ruched into hard peaks.

His mouth watered as he considered how best to warm her breasts up again.

He levered himself out behind her as she bundled herself into the robe, covering up all that delicious flesh, then stamped her feet back into the sliders and rushed down the deck towards the sauna cabin.

He was still laughing, the adrenaline making him even more euphoric than usual as the door of the cabin slammed shut behind her.

He tugged on his own robe, his skin brilliantly alive from the cold, but his groin pulsing hot with a very different kind of vitality. He entered the large wooden cabin he had built several summers ago, stoked the fire, added a few more logs so they could stay inside for a while, then ducked into the sauna.

She sat on the top bench, shivering, despite the dry heat—the robe still wrapped tightly around her naked body.

Well, now, that wouldn't do.

He dropped his own robe, kicked off his sliders aware of the thick ridge in his wet shorts as the raw heat poured through his system now on the tails of the adrenaline overload.

'How the…?' Her brows rose in astonishment as her gaze snagged on the proof of his need. 'How can you possibly be hard again? After that?'

'Because I am always hard for you,' he said, his chuckle roughened by the familiar desire, although his heart stuttered at the realisation it was only the truth.

He placed his foot on the bench below her to ease the robe off her shoulders. 'Can you not feel it too? The rush?'

Her fingers released their death grip on the flannel and she let him cast the robe aside—to reveal the flushed flesh he adored. Her gaze met his, the depth of emotion making his heart stumble, when she nodded.

'Yes, it's…' She breathed in, the motion making her breasts lift, drawing his gaze to the puckered nipples, so taut and ready it was as if they were begging for his mouth. 'I'd forgotten how good it feels, to swim outside in cold water. The rush afterwards is incredible,' she said, the wistful look in her eyes enchanting him.

'You have been ice swimming before?'

'Not exactly.' She chuckled, the sound light with pleasure. Her full lips curled, making her whole face brighten. 'There's a beach near my family's farm in Wexford called Curracloe. Miles of sand and dunes. I used to swim there as a girl with my brothers.' She closed her eyes, let her head fall back, the memories lighting her face like sunshine.

'We'd go all year round,' she continued as he listened intently—riveted by this glimpse into her past, her childhood. 'Sneak down after school before we had to do our chores. It was the perfect escape. The winter was the best time, even though the surf was brutal. The water was warm into November, and there'd be no tourists, you see. We'd have the whole beach to ourselves. But then...' She paused, and something stark flashed across her features—taking the sunshine away. Her gaze had lost the golden glow of memory, her expression becoming bleak when she opened her eyes.

'But then what?' he probed, even though he knew it was dangerous to ask. Dangerous to care about what had put the sadness in her eyes. Dangerous to want to know where that bleak look had come from.

'It doesn't matter.' She shrugged and smiled. But the innocent joy was gone.

She pressed her palm to the thick ridge in his shorts. 'Perhaps we should take care of this now you've revived me,' she added provocatively.

His aching flesh leapt to her touch. But he knew a distraction technique when he saw one.

He clasped her wrist, dragged those tempting fingers away.

'Tell me,' he said as he sat beside her on the bench. He pushed the wet locks of her hair back so he could see her face. 'Why did you stop swimming as a girl?'

She sighed. 'The story is a passion killer.'

Nothing could kill his passion for her, he thought wryly. But he only said again, 'Tell me.'

Her shoulders hitched, but for once he did not become fixated on the bounce of her bare breasts.

'Da caught us one afternoon,' she said. 'And took a belt to my brothers and me. After that, there was no escape in it any more. Just the fear he would catch us again.'

'Your father hit you with a belt?' he asked, unable to hide his shock, not just at the revelation, but the lack of emotion in her tone when she revealed this ugly detail.

He knew enough about Cara Doyle to know she was not an unemotional woman.

She folded her arms across her breasts, the flush of shame in her cheeks making him want to punch a wall.

'The man was a brute,' she said, without any inflection at all. 'And I hated him. But to be fair, it was the only time he ever hit me. My brothers all felt the end of his belt on a regular basis. But he preferred to spend his time calling me a dirty whore.' She let out a half-laugh, but it had no humour. 'If he could have seen me this past week, jumping you every chance I get and enjoying every second of it, I've no doubt he would have considered himself right about that.'

The revelation disturbed him, but not as much as the flicker of shame in her voice, or the rush of anger that flared like wildfire. His fingers curled into fists. He wanted to kill the bastard. For putting that thought into her head.

Was this why she had not discovered sex before now?

Why she had reacted so strangely when they had made love the first time?

Had the ravings of a bastard made her believe it was wrong to enjoy the connection they shared?

He cupped her cheek, stroked his thumb over the pounding pulse in her neck.

'We have been jumping each other, Cara,' he murmured, suddenly desperate to show her what they had together was good, pure. Meant to be indulged. And never dirty.

'True.' Her lips lifted, but he could still see the conflicting emotions in her eyes. Pain, sadness, confusion.

He took her hand, pressed her palm to the thick ridge still making him ache. 'Let me show you why this is not dirty,' he said. 'Why he was always wrong.'

Her gaze filled with something he could not name... Wasn't sure he wanted to name. Something bold and sweet and unafraid.

But when she nodded, he was glad, because the shame was gone.

'Okay,' she said.

He eased her folded arms away from her breasts. Until she sat before him, her skin glowing, flushed from the heat, her nipples rigid with desire.

Lifting the swollen weight to his lips, he captured the taut peak and sucked it deep into his mouth. She groaned, and braced her arms on the bench behind her, offering herself to him as he kissed and tugged at the ruched flesh, knowing how to make her ache.

Desire flared through him as she dislodged his mouth from her nipple to ease down his shorts. She bent to capture the rigid erection in her lips with an enthusiasm he had always adored, but admired even more now.

She had conquered those demons, this week, with him. And he was glad.

He sat, shuddering, shaking, watching intently as she worked him with her mouth.

The passion built. Hard, fast. Until he was forced to grasp her cheeks, lift her from him.

He wanted this to be for her. Wanted to give her an orgasm that would obliterate the last of her father's lies. Until all that was left was the joy.

He dragged her off the bench, positioned her pliant body until she was bent over, her hands braced on the shelf. He held her hips, tugged down the shorts and eased into the tight wet clasp of her body from behind, knowing the penetration would be deepest from this angle. He let her take the full measure of him. The feel of her body contracting around his aching length was pure torture.

She groaned. 'Please, Logan, move.' Her whole body shuddered. 'It's too hot in here.'

He laughed at her double meaning. The sweat dripped from his brow onto her back as he stared at the place where they were joined. He wiped the moisture away. But shifted only slightly, to nudge the spot deep inside her he knew would drive her wild.

'Logan… For pity's sake…' she begged, tried to move, but he held her firmly for the deep stroking, rolling his hips, making her take only what he wanted to give.

He nudged, pressed, stroked… Torturing them both. Never taking her over, building the passion to impossible proportions.

The battle for control raged between them in fire and ice as the titanic climax hovered a whisper away. Too close and yet not close enough.

Until at last, her swollen flesh pulsed and shattered, massaging his length. Her throaty cry of release triggered his own vicious climax.

He pulled out, slammed back into her. Once, twice, until his own orgasm crested.

They lay sprawled together on the floor of the sauna moments later, the dry heat all but unbearable now as steam rose from their sweat-slicked bodies. He dragged her into his arms, pressed a kiss to her forehead.

'He was wrong, Cara,' he murmured. 'There is no shame here. Ever.'

She glanced up at him. The cheeky smile she sent him—tinged with the innocent joy that had always captivated him—made his heart leap painfully in his chest.

'I know. But when we get back to the house, you may have to give me another demonstration, just so I can be sure.'

He was still laughing while he washed off in the sauna bucket, dressed hastily and then raced her back to the house in the fading daylight—more than ready to prove his point all over again.

CHAPTER NINE

FOUR DAYS AFTER she and Logan had started ice swimming each morning, Cara sat at the kitchen table—spooning down some yoghurt and fruit—and stared at the note she'd found on the counter when she'd woken up alone.

Had to go out. Back later.
L

She swallowed down the bubble of disappointment and irritation. And the dumb ache in her throat.

Why hadn't he mentioned he was heading out when he'd woken her up just before dawn to make slow luxurious love to her while she was barely awake? She might have liked to go with him. And where exactly had he gone when the nearest town was Saariselkä—which had to be at least fifty miles away by her reckoning—and she knew he never went there?

Curiosity, and boredom, were the only reasons she would miss him today, she told herself. That and the fact she could not ice swim alone, something she had become addicted to in the last four days.

She folded the note and stuffed it into the pocket of her robe... Or rather *his* robe. Her body was still humming from their session before dawn, her nerve-endings tingling with awareness and that reckless passion—that unquenchable fire—that he could ignite so easily. Her frown deepened. Had he woken her deliberately, to exhaust her, so that she would be fast asleep again when he sneaked off for the day?

She swore. A curse word her mammy would have washed her mouth out with soap for using echoed off the granite surfaces.

Of course, he had. Which could only mean one thing. He still didn't trust her—not completely. Not enough to let her accompany him wherever he had gone today.

The hollow feeling of disappointment—that he'd abandoned her for the day so easily—expanded in her chest and pushed against her ribs. She pressed her fingers to her eyelids, annoyed even more by the sting of tears.

What was wrong with her? She didn't need him to trust her. She'd entered into this liaison with her eyes wide open.

Just sex. Not intimacy. Not companionship. Not by any means a relationship. It wasn't what he'd offered and it was what she had happily agreed to.

But...

The pressure in her chest, the sting of sensation making her eyeballs hurt, refused to subside. They'd spent the last ten days together, barely apart. And it hadn't been just about sex, not any more. Not for her.

'There is no shame here. Ever.'

The words he'd said to her in the sauna four days ago echoed in her head. As they had a hundred times since that moment, when everything had changed. She'd shared something with him she hadn't shared with anyone. The shame she'd carried with her for so long, without even really acknowledging it. And he'd somehow made it better. The ice swimming each morning now helping to reinforce her escape from that shame. That fear. That judgment.

He'd understood something she wasn't even sure she'd understood herself.

She'd always been sure she had got over her father's insults, had never internalised them. She had even been stupidly grateful that he'd only once used his belt on her the way he had so often used it on her brothers. Sticks and stones and belts were worse than names, she'd told herself.

But after feeling that rush on her skin again, after so long, from swimming in cold water, it had brought it all back. How she'd loved to go down to the beach with her brothers. How those stolen swims had been an escape, an act of rebellion, a secret pleasure they had all shared. The teasing and games, the larking about, even the shared misery as they'd scrambled back into their clothes in the howling wind, pressing sandy feet into damp shoes. Those swims had been a chance to get away from the miserable tension, the barely leashed violence, the cruel words and endless threats that had marred so much of their childhood. Those swims had allowed them to be children again.

And she'd missed it, unbearably, once it had been stolen from her. By their da.

So much so, she'd forced herself to believe she didn't need it. She didn't even want it anymore. The camaraderie with her brothers, the sweet rush of feeling, the stolen moments when they were just kids together— not hostages to her father's moods and binges, his violent, volatile temper.

And Logan had somehow understood that. And given it back to her.

He'd listened intently to her story. The good memories and the bad. And offered comfort, and validation. And even joy. With his words and then his body. And he'd reinforced that new-found freedom every day since, coaxing her to the *avanto* until she'd become as addicted to the rush as he was…

They hadn't spoken again about her past. But she'd begun to look forward to their mornings now as much as their nights.

But that was off the agenda today, because he wasn't here.

It wasn't just the swim. What was worse was the knowledge that the sense of connection, which had felt like so much more than sex—the new-found intimacy, the friendship she thought they'd built with the easy smiles, the playful gestures, the moments out of bed—couldn't have meant to him what they had to her.

Or he wouldn't have thrown away the chance to

swim with her today. When they only had a few more days left together.

She picked up her mug and bowl, carried them over to the dishwasher and loaded them in, breathing heavily so the pressure in her chest—that feeling of loss—wouldn't crush her.

Cara, lighten up. He promised you nothing. If you thought this could be more, perhaps it's good now you know for sure it can't be.

She braced her hands on the counter and watched the precious Arctic daylight bounce off the surfaces.

It was already close to noon. And she had no idea when he would be back. And when he deigned to return, would he be expecting her to be waiting for him, naked and willing, like a dutiful little sex object?

The anger and frustration at his high-handed decision not to give her a choice this morning to accompany him, not to stay and spend time with her, pushed the regret and yearning back. Mostly.

A shadow floated across the room and she spotted the snowy owl—which she'd seen several times before—soaring majestically over the frozen lake. Its large tawny wings spanned the air currents as it dipped and dived, then rose again, its predatory grace making her breath clog as a small creature struggled in its talons, before it disappeared into the towering birch trees that edged the lake.

She pushed away the stupid sense of loss. Why was she moping about? When she could be doing something she loved instead, but had neglected for over ten days now.

She'd thought about photographing the owl every time she'd seen it fly past in the last week, but she hadn't been able to act upon it. The weather had been an excuse until yesterday, but the truth was she'd got sidetracked—because her time with Logan had been so precious. And finite.

What an eejit she'd been.

She marched towards the bedroom. After donning her first two layers, she headed for the garage where she kept her outer clothes—and the camera she'd had packed away for too long, her fingers already itching to use it.

After she had zipped herself into the cumbersome snowsuit, and double-checked the camera, she shouted out the Finnish command Logan used to open the garage door and headed out into the newly fallen snow. Her boots made crisp indents in the drifts, as she walked past his snowmobile tracks and headed towards the forest, her strides purposeful. Determined.

He had asked her not to leave the house without him, but he wasn't here to stop her. Because he had chosen not to be. And she'd be damned if she would pass up the opportunity to study the owl and maybe capture it on film—and start reaffirming her priorities.

Logan turned off the snowmobile's ignition and ordered the garage doors closed. He stripped off his outer layers, then began unpacking the food supplies he had picked up from the regular air-drop location on the edge of his land—even though every instinct was telling him to race through the house and find Cara.

He'd spent a whole day away from her, to prove that he could—so he forced himself now to complete the mundane task.

In three days, she would be gone. And his life would have to continue as normal. That he would miss her—the feel and taste and scent of her in his bed— was something he needed to get a handle on.

Except it wasn't just the sex he would miss any more, he thought grimly as he unloaded and stacked the dry goods. Because the more he tried to focus on the physical, the more he found himself thinking about all the other things he would miss.

He'd avoided any more revealing conversations about her childhood since their first ice-swimming session, had stifled all the questions that remained lodged in his head. Because that would simply encourage more intimacy. And she might expect him to return the favour. To revisit parts of his own past he had no wish to discuss.

But the questions still haunted him.

How had she survived such a brutal upbringing? And become such a strong, independent woman? Forthright, bold, brave, and so open.

He had become addicted to swimming with her each morning since, seeing her duck into the water, seeing her grin when the rush hit, warming her up afterwards in the sauna…

It had become a ritual that he had woken up this

morning wanting so badly to keep that he'd known he had to leave her alone for the day.

But it had been torture to be without her during the long ride to the drop zone. How was he going to survive once she was gone for good? The chatter of her conversation in the evening as they cooked their supper? The sight of her first thing each morning, her hair a mess as she took that first gulp of coffee with an indulgent sigh? Her rouged skin as she shot out of the *avanto* with an ear-splitting shriek...

He breathed past the growing obstruction in his throat.

Damn it...

All the moments he had greedily stored in his memory would haunt him when she was no longer here.

He slammed the cargo trunk shut. Then unhooked the sleigh. But as he tugged the towing vehicle past the shelving unit where they kept their snowsuits, he paused and frowned.

Where were Cara's outer garments? He checked his watch. It was edging towards three o'clock, close to nightfall.

Had she gone out without him? He left the sleigh and shot up into the house to check.

'Cara?' he shouted. No answer.

He searched the living area, the downstairs guest bedroom, jogged up to his own bedroom. The bed had been remade. But there was no sign of her.

Eventually he headed to the basement complex. The gym, the workshop. He even checked the freezer room as panic began to wrap around his chest, making his heart pound harder.

He should not have left her here alone. What if she had gone swimming without him? Surely, she wouldn't be so foolish? But even as he thought it, he imagined her face, that sweet grin splitting her features the day before as she'd managed to spend longer in the freezing water.

He charged back to the garage—the panic choking him—and checked that all the snowmobiles were still there. All four were accounted for.

Even so, his breathing continued to accelerate. Where was she? It would be dark soon. What if she had got lost? She had no idea where she was. The lake could be treacherous, the forests even more so. The bears hibernated at this time of year, but sometimes there could be one—sick or injured that could not hibernate and would be starving, desperate for food. And then there were the wolves that hunted in packs on the other side of the gorge. They never ventured near the house, but what if they had spotted her and come to investigate…?

He dashed outside as the sun dipped beneath the treeline. The brittle daylight had turned to the glow of twilight. He found her tracks, veering away from the trail he had taken to the drop zone that morning. But the boot prints had already frozen. She must have left hours ago.

Visions of her broken bloodied body, lying in the snow, or floating frozen in the water, made his lungs contract, his breath seize in painful gasps.

'Cara?' he rasped, but barely any sound came out, the shout trapped in his larynx.

The silent screams drew him back to that night, so long ago, as he stumbled through the snow, his legs so heavy he felt as if he were being sucked back into the terrible nightmares that had all but destroyed him once.

Instead of the quiet crunch of his boots, all he could hear was torrential rain, hitting the broken sidewalk in waves. The dirty water washed over his mother's pale face, and red blood spread across the starched white cotton of his father's dress shirt, like the fingers of a corpse. The heavy weight on his back a burden he couldn't shake. Stifling. Suffocating.

The screech of an owl jerked him back to the present, forcing him to focus. To lock the nightmares back into the recesses of his mind where they belonged. A shape appeared in the distance, through the trees, and stood up.

'Cara,' he murmured, his voice a rasp of sound.
Not broken...whole.

The fear released its stranglehold on his throat, the trapped air expelling from his lungs, but as he charged towards her, needing to hold her, to make sure she was real, she was his, she was safe, he spotted the camera in her hands. And the frantic fear became a rush of fury.

CHAPTER TEN

'LOGAN, OVER HERE!' Cara shouted, and waved.

She'd seen him return ten minutes ago, the snow-mobile crossing the lake, and had struggled not to stop what she was doing instantly and rush to the house to greet him. Like a lovestruck fool.

He'd been gone the whole day. And she'd be damned if she'd give him the satisfaction of knowing how much she'd missed him.

Observing the owl and its nesting area, taking shots to document its habitat and flight paths, had managed to keep her mind off the feeling of rejection, of loss. Mostly... But she couldn't ignore the leap of exhilaration in her chest—or how much it scared her—as he trudged towards her.

But as he got closer, the exhilaration downgraded considerably.

He looked like he had when they'd first met. Maybe because his head was bare, the waves of dark hair dancing in the breeze, and without the balaclavas she could see the hard line of his jaw, the brittle expression.

'Hi,' she said, tugging down her face covering as a shiver racked her tired body.

She'd been out in the forest for a couple of hours and had noticed the discomfort a while ago. But each time she'd contemplated returning to the empty house, she'd decided to stay a little longer. The pictures she'd taken weren't great, but they had felt important somehow. A declaration of intent. A chance to regain her purpose after ten days of indulgence.

'You're back,' she added inanely, because he hadn't responded, the fierce expression on his face starting to bother her.

'You are freezing.' He grasped her arm and turned, dragging her back towards the house. 'How long have you been out here, putting yourself in danger?'

What the hell?

'Logan, let go.' She jerked her arm out of his grasp, almost dropping the camera. The sense of loss she'd been ruthlessly controlling all day was joined by a spurt of resentment, and fury. 'I wasn't in any danger. I'm less than a kilometre from the house. Not that you'd care anyhow—you've been gone all day who knows where.'

The minute she'd said the words, she wanted to snatch them back.

Really? Could she sound any more clingy?

Before she had a chance to contemplate the depths of her humiliation, though, or how he had managed to turn her into this pathetic creature she didn't even recognise, he bent and scooped her onto his shoulder.

'Logan, damn it, put me down,' she cried, thumping his broad back as he stamped back through the snow. Her fury quickly outpaced her humiliation as she kicked and twisted, but to no avail. The man was as strong as a damn ox—and twice as arrogant.

He had carried her like this before, the first time they'd been ice swimming, and she'd secretly loved it then, his strength, his determination and the playfulness beneath.

She wasn't loving it any more though, as she struggled to get free of his hold—but only exhausted herself more—while he carted her back to the house like an unruly child.

They were both panting when he finally dropped her on her feet in the garage.

His cheeks were flushed from the cold, and the exertion, his heavy breaths matching her own. But she could see the harsh expression and it sparked the feeling deep in her chest she remembered from her childhood… When her da had arrived home from work, or the pub, in the kind of mood they all knew would cause trouble. For everyone.

She'd cowered then. But she refused to cower now.

She wasn't a little girl any more. And Logan, for all his high-handed ways, was not her father. But even so, she felt the pressure in her chest, that hole in her stomach, caused by the feeling of inadequacy, of judgement, which had made her feel small in the face of a man's temper.

'How long were you out there?' he demanded again, as if he had the right to question her decisions. Her autonomy.

The fury burst free, incinerating the anguish.

She dragged off her head gear, the balaclavas and the goggles around her neck, and threw them at his chest. He ignored them.

But he couldn't dodge her outrage.

'You bastard!' she shouted as she shoved the camera in its box with clumsy hands and placed it on the ground. The camera he'd all but forbidden her to use. The camera he could have broken with his stupid stunt.

Once the camera was safe—no thanks to him—she ripped off her gloves, all five pairs of them, and threw them at him too.

He barely blinked.

'I was working.' She ground the words out to stop from screaming. She tore down the zip on her snowsuit, began to struggle out of the layers as he continued to glare at her as if he were her keeper. 'And I wasn't finished.'

She didn't care about his anger. It would be a cold day in hell before she cowered before a man ever again. Especially a man who had been gone all day, without a word of when he'd be back.

'It was getting dark,' he shouted back, his own voice rising—the stony expression belied by the fire in his eyes as he threw off his own layers. His pectoral muscles heaved beneath the clinging nylon of his thermal undershirt as he kicked off his boots, and his ski-pants.

The spike of awareness as his big body was revealed only infuriated her more.

'There are bears, wolves and also the threat of storms, like the one which brought you here,' he growled as if he were speaking to an imbecile, his anger making a muscle tic in his jaw. 'They come from nowhere without warning. Even a hundred yards from the house you would be in danger.'

'So what? How is that any of your concern?' she replied, the rage making her body heat spike, even though she stood before him now in nothing but her thermal tights and undershirt.

She saw the awareness shadow his gaze as it roamed over her. And felt the answering hum in her abdomen, that hot, melting sensation between her thighs that meant her body was readying itself for him. Even though she hated him in that moment. Or wanted to hate him. For making her feel like that girl again—scared of being chastised.

He glared at her. 'You know it is my concern. When you are here, you are mine.'

'Well, that's where you're wrong, fella,' she yelled back, hating the dark possessive look in his eyes, the way his gaze raked over her with a sense of ownership. And the way her heart hammered her ribs in heavy thuds because a part of her wanted it to be true. The weak, needy part of her she thought she'd destroyed long ago. 'I belong to no one but myself,' she said, determined to convince herself as much as him. 'And I'll not be taking safety advice from a man who lives in the middle of nowhere alone. And can't even deign to tell me where he's been.'

She turned on her heel, to march away, so furious

now—with herself and the stupid wayward emotions battering her—she was about to explode.

'Don't!' The low demand broke over her and reverberated in her chest, stopping her in her tracks.

Then his fingers grasped her arm and pulled her round. He pressed her back against the garage wall. His forehead touched hers, his staggered breathing hot on her neck, as he dragged her clumsily into his embrace. But then the hard ridge of his arousal pushed into her belly, making the heat flare at her core. She slammed her palms against his chest, determined to push him away, to deny that bone-deep yearning that had troubled her all day, and made her a woman she didn't recognise. A woman who needed his touch, his presence, his validation.

She struggled to get free of him—and the emotions that had sneaked up on her in the last ten days without warning, and which she had no clue how to navigate.

But then he murmured, 'Please, don't...'

She stilled, shocked by the raw plea in his voice.

'You had icicles on your lashes,' he said, his tone rough as he cupped her cheek, his hand warm against her chilled skin. 'I was scared you were dead.'

What?

She gripped his undershirt, registering the fear and anguish on his face.

'They died and I did nothing to save them,' he added, wild grief shadowing his eyes. 'I cannot lose you too.'

'Logan...?' she murmured, the last of her anger

deserting her, the distress in his voice crucifying her. 'What are you talking about?'

The pain flared in his eyes and she thought she understood. Was this about his parents? About what had happened all those years ago? A fear she had somehow triggered, because he cared for her, too. Enough to want to keep her safe.

Anguish for him tore at her chest—terrifying, but also somehow liberating. Because she felt so much less alone.

'Logan, is this about your parents? Can you tell me what happened to them?'

He shook his head. But as he pressed his forehead to hers again, and held her tight, emotion rippled through him and she understood he was scared to let her go.

She cradled his cheeks, looked into his eyes. 'It's okay, Logan. I'm okay. I'm safe. I was never in any real danger, do you understand?'

He nodded, then pressed his mouth to hers, silencing the questions. The surge of need that had been building all day rushed in. He kissed her with a frantic passion—as if reassuring himself that she was whole. That she was his.

Suddenly they were tearing at each other's clothes, desperate to reach flesh—as desire bridged the last of the gap between them.

This was simple, basic, she realised. A way to cope with the devastating emotions churning in her chest and making her heart hurt. The yearning she had worked so hard to suppress fed the frantic need.

Until he lifted her naked in his arms and impaled her on his thick shaft.

She sank onto the strident erection, taking him to the hilt in one long, slow, unbearable glide. Her swollen sex stretched to receive him as she had done so many times before. But this time, as he began to move in frantic bursts, her back thumping against the wall, her heart soared into her throat.

The pleasure slammed into her, and her sobs were matched by his harsh shout of release.

Afterwards, she clung to his shoulders, and buried her face in his neck.

'I am sorry, Cara,' he mumbled against her hair. 'I should not have left you alone.'

Her ragged breathing cut through the quiet air, but even the wave of afterglow couldn't hide the gaping hole in her chest that swallowed her whole at his gruff apology.

He carried her into the house, and up to the bedroom, as if she were precious, cherished. But as he tucked her into his bed, then joined her, pulling her into his arms, the plunging pain in her stomach returned.

Had she made a terrible mistake?

How could she have fallen so hopelessly in love with this difficult, taciturn, untouchable man—enough to want to ease his pain and find out where it had come from?

Enough to want to save him? Even though he hadn't asked to be saved.

He hadn't even asked her to stay, and if he did, how

could she accept? When it would surely mean giving up everything she'd worked for, everything she'd dreamed of, for a man... The way her mother had.

You couldn't save someone, couldn't change someone, who didn't want to be saved.

But as she lay warm in his arms, feeling the thumps of his heartbeat reverberating against her back, she recognised the well of hope that bubbled up under her breastbone.

She mattered to Logan, in a way no other person had for a very long time. And that had to be as scary for him as it was for her. Maybe even more so. But surely that also had to mean something?

Now all she had to do was figure out exactly what it meant. And whether she could nurture and protect the well of hope... And turn it into something more tangible.

In the three days they had left together.

No pressure, then.

'Who were you talking about yesterday, Logan? When you said they died and you could do nothing to save them?'

Logan's hand stilled on Cara's belly where he had been lazily stroking her. The warm heat from the sauna and the drugging feeling of sexual satisfaction had relaxed him and made him feel in control of his emotions for the first time since yesterday's argument.

But as he glanced up from the lower bench, to find her watching him, her face flushed from their latest swim and the traditional warm-up afterwards, he tensed.

Why had he thought she would not recall the things he had let slip last night while he had been blindsided by the old fear?

When he had woken this morning, to find her already up and keen to go swimming, he had assumed she had forgotten their argument. And when she had said nothing as they conducted their wake-up swim, he had convinced himself all would be well.

But as she stared at him now, her gaze probing, the questions in her eyes unleashed the intense emotion from yesterday all over again.

'Were you talking about your parents?' she said softly as she stroked his cheek. Coaxing, curious, compassionate.

He sat up, deliberately dislodging her hand, because he wanted so badly to lean into that consoling touch. And that would be bad.

He didn't want to revisit that night. Not again. Didn't want her to know about the fear that had broken him as a boy—and could break him again, if he let her in the rest of the way.

But as his mind raced, trying to figure out how to avoid her questions, how to deflect or ignore that look in her eyes, she added, 'Were you with them when they died, Logan?'

He flinched and shook his head, but he could see she had caught him in the lie. Because her expression was suffused with sympathy.

He stood, suddenly too exposed, too raw. He headed

for the door to the sauna. They were naked, sweaty, his groin still pulsing with the aftermath of his recent climax and he had few enough defences already when she looked at him that way.

'It's getting cold,' he said, by way of explanation, even though his face was burning as he entered the changing room and began pulling on his clothes.

He concentrated on adding the layers necessary to return to the house, aware of her following him into the room, and silently getting dressed too.

As he tugged on his gloves, he could feel the guilty flags lighting his cheeks.

After getting rid of their snowsuits and outdoor layers in the garage, they headed up to the living area, and made their breakfasts—him a traditional Finnish porridge and her a bowl of fruit and yoghurt—as the tension and guilt knotted in his gut.

He stole glances at her as he stirred the thick multigrain oatmeal on the stovetop, transferred it to a bowl and added slices of apple and a sprinkle of cinnamon, while she laid the table, and scooped yoghurt and frozen berries into a bowl then grabbed the coffee pot and poured them both a cup.

The domesticity struck him. And didn't help with the panic. When had he become so settled, so comfortable with her in his space? Enough to know he would miss her desperately when she was gone.

She didn't press him, didn't probe as they sat to eat, didn't say anything at all in fact. It annoyed him to realise he even missed the chatter she always used to fill the silence.

But something about her stoic acceptance of his refusal to engage in this conversation only tightened the knot in his gut, making each mouthful of the hearty porridge a chore instead of a pleasure.

She hadn't looked at him directly, not once, since he had walked out of the sauna.

Did she believe he owed her this information, because when he had asked about her past, she had confided in him? Was this some kind of pay-off? Some unspoken rule in relationships he knew nothing about?

But they didn't have a relationship, he told himself. *Except…*

What about yesterday's argument? Wasn't that exactly what a relationship was?

Angry words? Charged silences? Broken promises? And then the inevitable make-up sex. Wasn't what had happened yesterday very much like the little he could remember of his parents' relationship?

Although, he thought miserably, when he had made fast frantic love after their argument, and held her in his arms, he hadn't felt used, or bitter, he had felt calm, and settled… And safe.

He blinked, the porridge like cement paste now in his stomach.

But he didn't feel settled any more, or calm, he felt agitated, on edge. As if more than just his control was slipping through his fingers—and he had no clue how to hold on to it.

Finally, he couldn't swallow another mouthful past the thickness in his throat. He pushed the bowl away.

'Yes, I was there,' he blurted out. 'I asked them to

take me to the movie premiere that night,' he added, remembering for the first time details he had forced himself to forget.

He had begged to attend the new dinosaur movie, so he could boast about it to all his friends at the boarding school he attended in Boston. He rarely saw his parents—their social lives a whirl of high-profile events linked to his father's business interests and his mother's position as a former supermodel turned socialite. As soon as they had climbed into the limo together though, he had regretted the impulse, because his parents had started arguing.

The porridge turned over in his stomach as he remembered the cutting words, the furious whispers as the car had driven through lower Manhattan to the event. And he had sat staring out of the window, watching the rain pour down on the stormy October night, seen the people scurrying to get home along the sidewalks as he'd wished he could be anywhere but inside that car. With them.

He had so few clear memories of them. How strange he could now recall in such vivid details his unhappiness with them that night...

Cara's gaze connected with his at last. But the moment of relief, because she had looked at him again, was quickly destroyed when the shadow of sympathy darkened her eyes to a rich emerald.

She placed her spoon in her bowl and reached across to cover the fist he had clenched on the table with her hand.

'I'm so sorry, Logan,' she said softly. 'That must

have been very traumatic. You don't have to talk about it, if you don't want to.'

He dragged his hand free. And stared out of the window—but instead of seeing the brilliant white landscape all he could see was that grey alley behind the theatre, and the man with the gun shouting. And the weight on his back, as he lay broken and scared, too terrified to move.

He didn't want to talk about this, about any of it. He had never even confided in his grandfather, when the old man had asked about the nightmares, which had finally faded over time. Nightmares he had deserved. But after the way he had overreacted yesterday, freaking out when she had chosen to leave the house, he realised he owed her this much.

He forced himself to look at her again, to absorb the compassion in her gaze.

While a part of him wanted to bask in the tenderness he could see in her eyes, another part of him was terrified of needing it. Of taking another treacherous step out of the isolation that had protected him for so long… But somehow the truth spilled out regardless.

'The man with the gun was shouting, telling me to come with him.' He stumbled through the memories, thrown back to the night he had avoided for so long. 'But I couldn't move. I was hiding behind my father. My mother was screaming and then…' He sucked in a breath, hearing the pops, feeling the impact as his father's body slammed into him, the dead weight crushing him as he lay on the pavement. 'I couldn't breathe.' He drew in a harsh breath, his lungs tightening up again. How could the suffocating fear still be so vivid? 'Not for a long time.' He stared at her, willing her to understand. 'Not until my grandfather brought me here.'

But as she looked back at him, her eyes deep pools of emotion, it occurred to him that he'd never felt so much. Not through all the years of isolation. Not until he'd met her.

The panic was swift and unequivocal, forcing him to acknowledge a truth he had never faced until this moment.

'Maybe if I had done what that man asked, they might still be alive.'

Instead of the contempt he expected to see in her face though, the contempt he felt for himself, all he saw was compassion.

'Oh, Logan, that's madness,' she said so simply he wanted to believe her. 'Surely you must know you had no part in their deaths.'

He shook his head, scared to believe her now, because it only made him feel more defenceless, more exposed.

'Is that why you've been alone here for so long?' she asked, gently. 'Because you're punishing yourself for something that happened to you as a boy that you had no control over? Can't you see how wrong that is?'

The words struck his chest, piercing the armour-plating he had built with a lifetime of solitude. Of abstinence. Armour-plating that had numbed his pain for so many years but had never been able to protect him from the yearning, the wanting, when it came to her. He clenched his fists, rose abruptly from his chair, his legs weak, his body shaky. He hated that boy who had been treated like a victim by the media swarms, and she saw as a victim too. Because that boy had lain on the broken pavement, suffocated by fear and the sharp metallic scent of his father's blood and been too scared to move, too scared to get help. But what he hated more was the thought of becoming that boy again.

Confused, terrified, defenceless.

She stood too, and came to stand in front of him, her eyes brimming with tears. Tears he was sure now he did not deserve.

'Logan, please don't be scared,' she said, her voice breaking as she touched his cheek. 'But I think I've fallen in love with you.'

He jerked his head back, the leap in his heart at her words swiftly followed by that crippling fear. Visions swirled into his mind, so close to the surface now he couldn't control them at all any more... The sweet, sickening aroma of death and day-old garbage, the violent shouts, the pounding rain, the cold weight of his father's body.

'I have to work,' he said, his voice barely audible, the present and the past combining as the suffocating feeling pressed in on him, like cold water closing over his head.

He walked out, aware of her standing alone in the kitchen.

He stayed all day in the workshop, working on the eagle, determined to close himself off, to rebuild the wall he had relied on for so long, so he would never have to remember that night again, and his part in his parents' deaths.

But when he found her in his bed, after a day spent trying to contain the fear, control the yearning, she responded to his touch with fierce passion, gave herself up to the driving need with unquestioning generosity. And he knew there would be no going back to that time when he had been able to protect himself from the broken parts of himself with denial.

So he took what she offered, and tried to convince himself he could keep her, as long as he never let her see the broken boy again, who he was terrified now would always lurk inside the man.

CHAPTER ELEVEN

CARA CLUNG TO Logan as the snowmobile trundled over the packed snow. She had to keep her head tucked into his spine, the icy wind biting the few spots of exposed skin. And keep her eyes firmly closed, so as not to encourage the tears that had been locked inside her heart for the past two days.

She'd told him she was falling in love with him. And he'd walked away from her.

She'd spooked him. In fact, he'd barely spoken to her since that morning.

She shouldn't have blurted it out like that. Shouldn't have burdened him with her feelings. Especially as it was obvious now he did not share them.

She'd wanted to help him, the way he'd helped her. She'd seen his pain, his trauma, understood a little more about why he had lived alone for so long when he'd spoken of his parents' deaths in that flat, raw voice. And her heart had broken for him.

Logan Colton, for all his wealth and self-sufficiency, his strength of character and carefully controlled emotions, was terrified of life. Of love. Of feeling too much. Of becoming that terrified child again. She got that now.

But that didn't mean he loved her. Nor did it mean she could change the course he'd set for his life, especially if he didn't want to change it.

And by locking himself in his workshop for the last two days, he'd made that very clear.

She'd debated whether to stay in his bed, had considered returning to the guest room she'd slept in when she'd first arrived. But ultimately, she'd been unable to take that final step. Because it had seemed pointless and self-defeating.

If all they could have was the sex—she'd take it. But each time he made love to her without a word, thrusting heavily inside her, bringing her to one shimmering orgasm after another—teasing and tormenting and provoking her, using all the skills they'd learned together over the last two weeks as if he wanted to bind her to him—she'd felt him pulling further away emotionally.

And she'd let him. Because what right did she have to ask more of him than he was willing to give?

She had no idea where he was taking her now— because he hadn't told her and she hadn't asked. But when he'd told her to be ready to leave at noon this morning, she hadn't argued with him.

The journey seemed to go on for ever, giving her far too much time to think of how she could have done things differently.

But as she held him, far too aware of the tensing and flexing of his muscular body through the layers of winter clothing, she couldn't find an alternative narrative that would give her the result she wanted.

Maybe she'd been a fool to lose her heart so quickly to a man who guarded his own emotions so fiercely. But she couldn't regret it. The last two weeks had been life-affirming in so many ways. She had never realised until this past week how scared she'd been to risk a relationship, because of the way her father had behaved. She'd taken so many risks to make her career a reality, while all the time denying or burying her emotional needs. She wouldn't do that any more. She had so much to give, so much to discover. And Logan had been responsible for luring her out of hiding. Her heightened emotions were just something she would have to learn how to manage when this was over.

At last, the snowmobile climbed out of the forest and headed across another frozen lake system. As the sun dipped towards the treeline on the other side of the ice, it highlighted a structure built on the opposite bank. As they got closer, she realised it was an A-frame cabin, constructed in wood, with a deck that would sit over the water in the summer months. Woodsmoke trailed up into the turquoise sky from a chimney in the peaked roof, and the glass frontage sparkled in the dying light.

As the snowmobile headed towards the ridge, her heart sank. Was this where he intended to leave her? With strangers? But as they drew closer, no one appeared from inside the house.

Logan parked the snowmobile in front of a garage, then pushed up his goggles as he looked over his shoulder.

'We stay here tonight,' he said.

She hated the way her heart rose into her throat, the stupid bubble of hope that had never completely died expanding in her chest.

Maybe this wasn't the end after all? If they had one more night together?

He swung his leg over the machine and dismounted, then helped her down from the saddle. Her legs were stiff and cold after the long ride and she stumbled.

'Easy,' he said and scooped her into his arms.

She marvelled, not for the first time, at his strength as he carried her effortlessly into the house.

As soon as they entered the well-insulated room, he put her down. Warmth hit her tired body. A wood-burning stove blazed in the centre of the open-plan space—which was equipped with a small kitchen and rustic but finely made furniture. She recognised the work as Logan's.

She could see a mezzanine level with a beautiful hand-carved bed covered in an embroidered quilt. Solar-powered fairy lights glowed through the glass spotlighting a hot tub on a platform outside and making it look like an enchanted bower.

The whole place was impossibly romantic. Why had he brought her here?

As they shrugged off their layers, she tried to figure out what to say, where to begin.

'Who lives here?' she asked finally.

He sent her a quizzical look. 'It is mine. I built it.

I paid a contact to prepare it for us. There is stew for tonight and wine.'

'But why?' she asked.

Today was supposed to be their last day together. Was this a farewell, or more than that?

The bubble of hope died though, when he stripped off the last of his outer layers, and she noticed the prominent ridge in his ski-pants—which was always there when they were together, it seemed.

Of course, he'd brought her here for one more night of 'exploring their sexual connection'—which had been his purpose all along. She was the one who had lost sight of that, not him. She was the one who had wanted to build more than just a sexual relationship.

'There is something I wish for you to see,' he said, cryptically. But then he picked up the camera case she had brought in with her and pulled out her Leica. 'Do you have space on the memory card?'

She frowned, surprised to see him handle the camera without sneering. She nodded. She'd spent the last few days checking through all the shots and deleting any she didn't wish to download when she returned to Saariselkä.

'Good,' he said. And passed her the camera. 'You will need it.'

He strolled to the kitchen area and produced a casserole dish from the fridge. He set it on the woodburning stove. After stoking the fire, he peered out across the lake at the gathering darkness. 'We have an hour before it's dark enough.'

For what?

Before she could ask, he added, 'Do you want to use the hot tub while we wait?'

The intensity in his gaze, the dark arousal in those pure blue eyes, warm now with a need he couldn't hide, told her all she needed to know about what he planned to do to her there. Perhaps she should say no, tell him she wanted a clarification of where they stood. Was this their last night or wasn't it?

But somehow, she didn't want to ruin this new truce. Didn't want to think about the future. She was tired of pondering what might have been. Wouldn't it be better to stay in the now? To enjoy the moment, to enjoy what they *did* have, and live the pipe dreams she'd weaved about them one last time before they could be dashed tomorrow? They'd built something precious over the past two weeks. Even if it was only a sexual connection for him it was so much more for her. And here was her chance to own it and enjoy it for a few more hours at least.

She loved him. And she didn't want to hurt him. Didn't want to press and probe at wounds that clearly hadn't healed. And might never heal.

She forced a smile to her lips, grasped his shoulder and bounced into his arms. He grunted and caught her, the fire in his eyes dancing as she wrapped her legs around his waist.

'Absolutely, but only if you join me there.' She swept her gaze over the dramatic sweep of his brows, the high cheekbones and day-old stubble that made him look so breathtakingly wild and untamed.

You tamed him for two whole weeks, Cara Doyle. And he's still yours tonight.

'Try to keep me away,' he said and let out a gruff laugh as he captured her lips with a hunger she adored, as if no other woman existed.

Was it any wonder she'd fallen for this bold, unknowable, insatiable man—who made her feel so alive and unashamed?

As he tugged off the last of her clothing and his own, then carted her outside and dropped her into the gloriously hot water, she forced herself to revel in the moment, to let the snow-laden beauty of the forest night add to the adrenaline rush of making love to him in the crisp winter light, and not to think of the empty space in her chest.

Or what tomorrow might bring.

'There, can you see them?' Logan whispered, pointing over Cara's shoulder, feeling her body still beneath his as they lay in the hide he'd built especially to view the wildlife a few years before. A hide he had never imagined wanting to share with anyone.

Her awed gasp had emotion tightening his ribs as she spotted the wolves silhouetted against the leap of coloured lights on the forest ridge. Turquoise blue and a flicker of iridescent pink edged the pulsing emerald as the aurora borealis swirled and shimmered, cutting across the inky, star-studded night and providing the perfect backdrop to the hunting pack.

'Oh, Logan, that's... Absolutely stunning,' she murmured. 'They're all white.' He could feel her excitement as she lifted the camera to her face and began clicking off shots from their vantage point. 'I've never seen a pack like it before. Are they all albinos?'

'No, they are a rare subspecies, all but extinct now,' he murmured.

His grandfather had told him as much when he'd spotted a pack like this as a teenager.

Wolf populations were growing in the south and east of Finland, with around two hundred of them now living in the wild—the tourist board even arranged photography trips so visitors could view them. But no one would ever see these wolves—and he'd wanted her to have this.

The alpha female paused and turned as if sensing their presence, then stretched her head towards the sky and howled, galvanising her pack for the hunt as a moose crashed through the trees in front of them, obviously scenting the wolves' presence. For several seconds, the lead wolf's snowy fur—usually camouflaged by the winter landscape—was aglow with the green and blue lightshow above her.

The natural wonder of the wolf though was nothing compared to the sight of Cara, eagerly photographing her and her pack. Not to Logan. He lay still and watched her face, the slight frown of concentration, the ice that had formed on her lashes as they waited, the glow of excitement in her eyes lit by the Northern Lights as she worked tirelessly to capture the pack before they dashed past the ridge chasing their prey.

He thought of the sight of Cara earlier in the hot tub, as she rode him, her body bowing back, her skin alive with sensation, her face a picture of ecstasy as she came. And later as he washed her in the cabin's shower and she gave herself to him again, without holding back. And without demanding more from him.

And he knew he couldn't lose her, couldn't let her go. Not yet.

The pack and their prey disappeared into the trees, and she flopped over onto her back, her face lit by the ethereal lights of the Lapland night.

She lifted her gloved hand to his face, her eyes glowing with achievement. 'Wow, Logan. Just wow,' she whispered, her voice muffled by her scarf. 'Thank you for giving me this.'

He could see the love and trust that had scared him so fundamentally two days ago. And suddenly he knew how to make her stay. What he could give her without exposing himself any more than he already had.

There was a way to make this work. All he'd had to do was find it.

He nodded and pressed a kiss to her nose. Then crawled out of the hide and dragged her out with him. 'Come, it is time to eat. And get warm again,' he said, eager to get back to the cabin and tell her his plan.

His heart skipped a beat when she laughed and murmured, 'Oh, goody. Getting warm with you happens to be one of my favourite pastimes.'

'If you stay with me, there is much you can photograph. The wildlife on my land has been untouched for generations.'

'Stay? With you?' Cara murmured as she placed the wine glass on the small table at the side of the bed, shocked not just by Logan's offer, but the casual way he made it.

She turned in his arms, so she could see his face, the harsh planes and angles lit by the firelight below them.

They'd made love again after supper, long, slow, lazy love, her excitement at the shots she'd taken only tempered by the thought of what the morning would bring. But as they'd sat on the bed, her wearing his boxer shorts and an undershirt, him in just his shorts in the warm room, sipping the last of the bottle he'd produced to go with the stew, she'd been unable to keep the empty space at bay.

Until this moment.

Anticipation dried her throat.

But then he nodded, placing his own glass beside hers, cupping the back of her neck, and brushing his thumb over the thundering pulse point.

'Yes. Stay,' he said.

The wave of emotion gathered in her chest then barrelled through her tired body. She'd hoped for such an offer, but she hadn't really expected it.

'I cannot lose you,' he said, the emotion in his voice matching her own as his eyes searched her face. This wasn't just hunger, it was affection, caring, much more than a physical connection just as she'd hoped. 'Not yet.'

Not...*yet*?

The single word echoed through her, bringing a discordant note to the symphony of joy and excitement.

The bubble in her chest deflated as what he was really offering her became clear. A relationship on his terms. An arrangement such as the one they already had, which involved her living a life of exile—and never probing too much, so he never had to face his demons.

'What do you say, Cara? Will you come home with me?' he asked, taking her hand in his and lifting her trembling fingers to his lips.

The yes lodged in her heart sat on the tip of her tongue as he kissed her palm. But somehow, she couldn't seem to utter it.

She tugged her hand free and fisted it in her lap, shifting away from him on the bed, suddenly knowing she couldn't give him what he wanted, or she would lose herself in the process.

'I… I don't know if I can,' she said, hating the words and the need to say them.

'Why not?' he asked, tilting his head to one side as he studied her, the way she'd seen him study one of his sculptures. As if she were a puzzle to be solved. 'You would be able to build your career as a photographer. Is this not what you want?'

'But how? How would I be able to show my work or sell it, even?' she asked.

It wasn't just that his home was isolated, that he had no Internet as far as she knew. He hadn't left his land in years. But more specifically, he hadn't let her in, not really.

She didn't expect him to give up his isolation. Nor did she expect a declaration of undying love.

They'd only known each other for two weeks. And she knew the last fortnight had been tumultuous for him too, as well as her. Maybe *too* tumultuous.

But she needed something, a sign that there could be more eventually. That he was committed to making this a real relationship, at some point in the future. That he was prepared to bend for her, too? That he wouldn't close her out of his heart for ever.

'There are ways, we could figure it out,' he said. 'I sell my work to a gallery in New York through a subsidiary.'

'But I would have to leave occasionally, Logan. The wildlife here is incredible and I would love to spend time observing it and photographing it, but if I'm really going to make a career, a living, out of my work I can't limit myself to one location.' She sighed. 'Especially not while I'm trying to establish myself. And I'd want to go to Ireland to see my family, too.' Maybe she hadn't been to see them in over a year, but did he realise what he was asking of her? 'Is that what you want?'

He frowned and she could see he hadn't considered the ramifications of what he was offering her. And what he wasn't.

'I have a lot of money, Cara…' He huffed out a breath. 'You would not need to support yourself, while you were with me,' he said. 'There would be no need to leave. And if you must see your family, I would figure out how to do that.'

Her heart broke at the rough emotion in his voice. And the dark intensity in his eyes.

'It's not about money, Logan.'

His frown deepened. 'Then what is it about?'

She got off the bed, wrapped her arms around her waist as she stared out into the night. The Northern Lights still flickered on the horizon, the magical play of colours over the forest so beautiful it hurt.

But the life he lived here wasn't a real life. Not for her. She would tumble the rest of the way in love with him, sink so deep she could never get out again. He would bind her to him, with sex and affection—something she had yearned for without even realising it—and she would want to save him. Just as her mother had once wanted to save her father, from the demons that had turned him into a cruel and bitter man.

Logan wasn't cruel or bitter. He was a good man, even a tender man in his own way. Forceful and possessive in another. But he was a damaged man.

A damaged man who had no desire to face his demons either. She wasn't even sure he understood that he had demons too. How much good would she really be doing him by helping him avoid them?

She heard him come off the bed behind her. He stroked her hair, then banded his arms around her waist and pressed his face into the back of her neck.

She leaned back against him, because she couldn't seem to stop herself.

It felt so good to be in his arms, so right. But how could it be, when he was still hiding from the world, and he wanted her to hide too?

'Don't complicate this, Cara, when it can be simple,' he said. 'You said you loved me, why is this not what you want?'

She spun round, her heart cracking open in her chest at the forthright expression on his face. 'Logan, you have refused to talk to me for two days… And you still can't bear to be around people. Can't you see why that's a problem?'

'No.' He shrugged. 'Because all that matters is that I can bear to be around you.'

She pushed her hair out of her eyes, agitated now, and heartsore. And desperately frustrated with the intractable expression on his face. He wasn't listening to her, because he chose not to.

'But can't you see, if I went back with you, if I lived with you, I'd want to talk about everything,' she said, trying one last time to make him understand. 'Because I'd want to know you, *really* know you.' She cupped his cheek, felt the muscle bunch under her palm as he stared back at her. 'Not just who you are now, but also that little boy, who you're still punishing.' He flinched, but she forced herself to continue. 'And I'd want you to know me. All my flaws and weaknesses. As well as my strengths. Because love is curious and demanding, emotionally as well as physically. Can't you see that?'

He placed his hand over hers, pulled it away from his face then said softly, 'Why does it need to be, when what we have is already so good?'

Good for you, she thought, and the ripple of bitterness was surprising, but there, nonetheless. Couldn't he give her anything? Not even an indication that with time things might change?

'You're asking me to give up too much, Logan. I'd lose myself, and my independence. One day, I might want to have children, a family of my own…' It wasn't something she was thinking of right this minute, but when she felt him stiffen, she suddenly understood. He wasn't going to budge about any of it.

'*Might* is not important,' he said, grasping her elbow, pulling her against his body. 'Nothing in life is guaranteed. We have only the now. What we feel, what we want. And I want you and you want me. That is enough.'

It was hopeless. Logan was a fatalist, a man bound to his past. Who couldn't break those chains. Wasn't even prepared to attempt to break them.

'I can't live like that, Logan, I won't.'

'Really?' he asked. 'You would deny us both this?' he said, then covered her mouth with his, kissing her with the furious hunger she recognised. And responded to always.

Her body quickened as he grasped her bottom, thrust the thick erection in his shorts against the melting spot between her thighs, rubbing her clitoris with expert intensity through the thin layers of cotton. His fingers sank beneath the waistband of her shorts, finding the slick nub and working it with ruthless efficiency.

She gasped, sobbed, the brutal climax already too close.

'You are wet for me, always, Cara,' he said, his

lips devouring her throat as she rode his fingers, unable to deny his mastery over her body. Or the tearing pain in her heart.

Somehow she managed to scramble back, to push him away. 'Don't, Logan.'

He stopped instantly, his face flushed, his eyes dark, the muscle in his jaw clenching.

'It won't work, not again,' she said, even as her body yearned for him. 'Sex isn't the answer—not this time. I need more than that. If you can't give it to me, that's okay. I understand. But I can't stay with you on your terms.'

He grunted as pain slashed across his face. He turned away from her, to stare out at the night sky, his arms crossed over his broad chest, his breath heaving. Everything inside her gathered. The stupid, foolish hope building again. Maybe, just maybe, she had broken through to him, to the man she suspected lay beneath that wall… The man she'd had tantalising glimpses of over the past two weeks. The man who enjoyed her company, who wanted to please her, and protect her, who she knew would be lonely without her… The man who had denied himself so much because he blamed himself for his parents' deaths.

But as the seconds ticked past, she saw the veil come down again. His breathing evened out, and his arms relaxed, to fall back by his side. And when he finally turned back towards her, the need, the desperation, the confusion were gone, until all that was left was the same implacable mask—tinged with impatience and frustration—she remembered from when she had first met him. He had retreated back into the shell where she couldn't reach him.

He nodded. 'I will sleep downstairs. We can talk again in the morning.'

It was a dismissal. Maybe even an ultimatum. But as he walked away, picking up his clothing to take the stairs to the living area below, she didn't stop him.

Talking more tonight was pointless. She was over-emotional. And they were both on edge, both tired, and when you factored in that endless hunger that never seemed to die between them, and his determination to use it against her... She wrapped her own arms around her body as she heard him making up a bed for himself on the sofa downstairs.

She crawled under the embroidered quilt, curled up in a ball, taking in a lungful of his clean fresh scent, bergamot and pine, rubbing her thighs together to ignore the sensation still humming at her core, where he had touched her with such purpose, such skill.

The low howl of a wolf in the distance cut through the crackle of the fire from downstairs and the thunder of her own heartbeat as she closed her eyes. And squeezed them tightly shut around the stinging tears.

Maybe tomorrow, once they'd both slept, she could reason with him again. She wasn't giving up, not yet. Not entirely.

But her heart felt unbearably heavy, as she finally drifted into a fitful sleep.

CHAPTER TWELVE

*Your snowmobile is in the garage. It is fuelled
and has a GPS to guide you to Saariselkä. Leave
early and do not travel at night. If you change
your mind, I will be waiting.*

*Contact Grant.Andrews@ColtonCorp.com and
he will arrange everything. But until then tell no
one of our time together.*
    Logan

A TEAR BURNED Cara's cheek as she stared at the note
left on the coffee table. She brushed the moisture
away with her fist. The empty living area, which had
seemed so romantic last night, now felt vacant and
oppressive.

She walked onto the deck and spotted the empty
space where Logan had parked his snowmobile the
day before.

Logan was gone. He must have left early, before

she had woken up. And all she had of him now was this curt message.

Hopelessness opened like a black hole in the pit of her stomach.

If you change your mind, I will be waiting...

A part of her wanted desperately to cling to that phrase. He had given her a chance to rewrite last night's argument—and get to the outcome they both wanted. To be together.

But as she sucked in an unsteady breath, trying desperately not to dissolve into tears, the pain in her chest refused to ease.

Because he hadn't given them a chance. Not really. What that phrase really meant was either you do this on my terms, or not at all.

But it was worse than that, because she knew the next few days and weeks, even months, were going to be torture—as she forced herself to resist his invitation.

She was going to miss him, so much. Miss him and the intense time they had spent together. Alone. In his stunning home on the edge of the world.

Not just the moments when he had given her more pleasure than she had realised she was capable of, hell, had even known existed before he had touched her, and tasted her. But also, those moments out of bed, as they prepared meals together or enjoyed the silence. The rush of ice swimming with him. Even the passion and anger of the arguments they'd had felt more real, more intense, than anything she'd ever experienced. She'd miss his home, too, that open, airy space, which should have felt like a prison, but never had. She'd loved the moments when she simply took the time to absorb the stillness, watching him work with those capable, skilled hands, carving something beautiful and compelling from the wood. The husky rumble of his voice as he teased or cajoled her, discovering a boyish side to his nature she was sure he'd never realised was there before her.

They had been good for each other. In so many ways. Because Logan hadn't been the only one living in isolation. The only one who had been lonely and alone before they'd met.

She left the note on the table, swallowing past the huge constriction in her throat. And let out a shout of frustration—that no one could hear but her.

Damn it, how could she hate him and love him at the same time?

She forced herself to put on her outdoor layers, to douse the fire in the wood burner, and leave the cabin, closing the door behind her firmly—even if she knew she would never be able to close out all the memories.

She found her snowmobile in the garage—repaired, just as he had promised her two weeks before. It occurred to her he must have arranged to have the machine brought here so he could avoid having anyone visit his home...

But when?

Had he always intended to use his invitation as an ultimatum? To discard her if she didn't agree to his terms? Or had last night's invitation been an impulse that he had regretted?

She opened the garage door, climbed onto the machine. As soon as she turned the key in the ignition, the well-oiled hum of the engine—so different from the ominous rattle it used to have whenever she started it—suggested no expense had been spared making it roadworthy again.

She gulped down a sob. Why did the thought of the effort he had made to prepare for her departure only make this that much harder?

She shoved the goggles down, twisted the accelerator and drove the machine out of the garage. She turned on the GPS tracker attached to the machine's handlebars.

Three hours, the route said.

But somehow she knew it would take her a great deal longer to leave this cabin, this forest, and her time with Logan Colton behind. Maybe even for ever.

As she headed south, following the route round the lake, past the place where they had huddled together waiting for the wolfpack the night before, she felt a part of her heart being torn away, and left behind her bleeding in the snow…

She arrived at the outskirts of Saariselkä nearly four hours later. Night was already closing in. The lights that lit the resort town made the snow-covered streets sparkle. She was exhausted, in mind and body and spirit, as she pulled up to the hotel where she had been working before she'd left two weeks ago to photograph the lynx. But as she turned off the ignition and dragged her camera box out of the saddlebag, she no-

ticed the flashing lights of several police cars and one
of the forest ranger's trucks parked by the entrance.

Odd.

The region only had a small police presence, and
the nearest station was over two hours' drive away.
She didn't think she'd ever seen a local cop in the town
the whole six months she'd lived here.

She trudged to the hotel's entrance, but as she
ripped off her head coverings on entering the building,
the warmth enveloping her, she spotted a tall man with
dark wavy hair standing by the reception desk flanked
by a couple of policemen and the local ranger. His
voice hit her first as he remonstrated with the cops.

Recognition streaked through her. 'Kieran?' she
gasped. What on earth was her oldest brother doing
in Lapland?

He swung round.

'Cara!' He rushed towards her, then grasped her
arms, the wild panic in his eyes making her touch
his cheek. To soothe. Kieran was a rock, he never
got over-emotional, but right now he looked a wreck.

'You're here, you're okay,' he murmured as the
police followed him across the lobby. As well as a
middle-aged woman, who began to snap photos with
her phone.

'What's wrong, Kieran?' she asked, frantic herself
now. 'Is it Mam?'

'No. Are you mad?' He swore, the panic turning
to fury in a heartbeat. 'It's you. We've been searching for you for days now. You didn't call Mam for two
weeks. We were frantic.'

'But I told her, I was taking time out to work on my portfolio,' she said, her mind reeling.

She usually called her mammy once a week, but she'd missed the scheduled phone call before. It had never occurred to her that her family would take on so.

'But where have you *been*?' he shouted, his fingers digging into her biceps, as if he was scared to let her go in case she disappeared. 'They found no trace of your vehicle and you haven't been back here in over two weeks.'

'Miss Doyle…' The older of the two policemen—who had a bold silver strip on his dark blue snow-suit—intervened. 'We began the search two days ago, at your brother's request. We were about to bring in the army,' he added in perfect English, despite the Finnish accent. 'Can you tell us where you have been residing over the past sixteen days? Have you been kept against your will?'

'No, I… No, I haven't been kept against my will,' she said, evasively, remembering Logan's request. She didn't want to reveal his whereabouts. To anyone.

But then the policeman frowned and her brother said, 'Then where the hell have you been, Cara? Because we know you haven't been here.'

'I… I can't tell you,' she managed. Her brother swore, while concern darkened the policeman's penetrating stare.

'Why can you not tell us, Miss Doyle?' he asked again, in that patient tone.

'I just… I can't say, but I was fine. Really. It was my choice.'

'Cara, this is nonsense,' her brother announced, his temper igniting. Although she didn't blame him. He must think there was something up.

'Mr Doyle, you must remain calm,' the policeman added. 'Your sister is well and found. These are just follow-up questions that—'

'Were you with Logan Colton, the sole heir to the Colton empire?' The probing question shot out of left field, but the guilty blush had suffused Cara's face before she could even register it had come from the woman who had been hovering nearby and was still taking photos.

'I… I'm not answering that,' Cara blurted out, then realised how incriminating that sounded. Her answer only seemed to encourage the woman—who Cara suddenly realised had to be a reporter.

'What's he like, Cara?' The journalist clicked an app on her phone then shoved it in Cara's face, her eyes glowing with excitement. 'Is his home as stunning as they say? Is *he*? You know he hasn't been seen in public since he was a boy of ten? And he witnessed his parents' brutal murder.'

'Get away with you,' Kieran announced, trying to shield Cara from the woman's aggressive questioning, just as the policeman took her other arm.

'Miss Doyle, let us take you to a more private place,' he said, but as he led her away she knew it was already too late. The reporter was dictating the exclusive story into her phone—throwing out words like 'billionaire recluse' and 'kidnap victim' and making Cara want to fold in on herself and disappear.

The exhaustion and sadness clamped down on her heart, making her feel even more alone, and far away from Logan. As if she'd travelled a million miles today, instead of under a hundred.

She would never be able to go back to him now.

Why hadn't she tried harder to win his trust? Before she had betrayed it so comprehensively?

The story broke in the Finnish press the next morning, and had been splashed all over the Internet by lunchtime. By nightfall, the hotel in Saariselkä had been besieged by photographers and reporters and celebrity journalists from all over the globe, trying to get an interview or even a glimpse of the woman who had been 'trapped in Colton's love nest' or 'kidnapped by a reclusive billionaire' or 'the first clue in decades to a billionaire enigma' depending on your news source of choice.

The whole thing felt unreal to Cara. Only twenty-four hours ago she'd been in Logan's arms. And now it felt as if her life had become disconnected from reality, because she was sleepwalking through a nightmare she couldn't escape.

Knowing that she was the focus of a media storm—that she couldn't even leave the hotel—was only one aspect of the nightmare though. Because her appearance from nowhere, after two weeks in the wilderness, had triggered a hunt for the location of Logan's home.

He'd managed to stay safe from scrutiny by keeping under the radar. There had been whispers that he was living in Finland, but nothing concrete, and she knew what lengths he'd gone to, to keep it that way. Now she had effectively outed him by default, she knew he would not be able to stay hidden for much longer—without hiring an army to protect himself, and that would defeat the purpose because he would no longer have his solitude.

She felt sick to her stomach, had been unable to eat or sleep for twenty-four hours. But even so, she had refused to talk to the police. Logan had done nothing wrong, and neither had she, so she owed them no more of an explanation than she owed the press.

Eventually the police had left.

Her brother Kieran, however, had been far more persistent.

'Why won't you talk to me, Car?' he said, stalking across the suite she had been given by the hotel for her own protection.

'*If* he didn't hurt you,' Kieran added, raking his hair with impatient fingers, '*if* he didn't kidnap you, why won't you tell me what happened while you were with him?'

She'd told him nothing, she hadn't even mentioned Logan's name, but that hadn't stopped Kieran from jumping to all sorts of ludicrous notions.

'I'm not talking about it, Kieran, because it's none of your business. Nor is it anyone else's. It's private.'

'He's one of the richest men in the US. ColtonCorp has been a *Fortune 500* company for two generations. If he exploited you, we should demand compensation. Damages.'

She jumped up from her seat by the window, where

she had been watching the press horde amassing all day. 'We'll demand nothing from him. He owes me nothing. He saved my life, so I'll not be paying him back by suing him,' she cried out.

'So you *were* with him. The reporter had the right of it.' Kieran's eyes narrowed.

Her bastard brother had tricked her into admitting the truth.

She slumped back in the armchair. Defeated. 'If you say his name to anyone, Kieran, I'll murder you,' she hissed, but she could hear the weary resignation in her own voice.

Enough to know it was an empty threat. She was too tired, too devastated to do anything.

He knelt down beside her armchair, rested his hands on the arms of the chair. 'Just tell me, Cara, did he hurt you?'

She shook her head, wiped away a tear. A pointless, self-pitying tear. 'No. He saved me, I told you.'

'Then why are you crying?' he asked, his voice gentle now, coaxing and full of the concern that made her feel like a little girl again, after being called names by their da.

Kieran had always been the one to come and tell her it meant nothing. To hold her and keep her safe. But as she turned to him, wanting to be held, to be reassured, she knew the only person who could do that now was Logan.

And he would never want to see her again. Not when the swarms of reporters and photographers found his home—which was surely only a matter of time.

'Because I love him, and I've destroyed his life,' she said simply.

She would have to leave Finland. The longer she stayed here, the more the story would grow. She'd had a lot of lucrative offers to buy her photographs, but she knew every one of them had nothing to do with the quality of her work and everything to do with her new-found celebrity—which meant she couldn't and wouldn't accept any of them.

By leaving Logan, she had destroyed the career she had been so determined to save. It would be ironic, if it weren't so pathetic.

'Hey, sis,' Kieran murmured, pulling her into his arms and holding her as the sobs began to rack her body. The sobs she'd held in ever since the long drive back to Saariselkä. 'Don't take on so. None of this is your fault.'

Except it was her fault. She'd been a coward, scared to trust her love. Scared to give them a chance, scared to believe Logan could change, if she gave him time. And now he never would.

CHAPTER THIRTEEN

Three weeks later

'CARA, HEY. HAVE you seen today's headlines? Yer man is back in New York. It's all over the news.'

Cara lifted herself off the rocky ledge to see her middle brother, Connor, running up the bank towards her waving his mobile phone.

Her heart jolted in her chest. Her eyes burned.

Logan. He had to be talking about Logan.

She'd been avoiding the news ever since the press had finally left her alone, convinced at last that she had no intention of giving any exclusive interviews. And once 'Colton's Secret Lair' had been uncovered in Lapland, the press had switched their attention back to Finland.

So, Logan had finally been forced to return to the US, the place where he had only bad memories. Probably for his own safety.

Anger roiled in her gut, right alongside a wave of guilt. What gave those vultures the right to change his life? To force him out of his home? His sanctuary?

'I'm not interested, Connor,' she said, trying to convince herself it was true. 'He's not my man.' And he never really had been.

Connor let his phone drop, his breath heaving after the run up the hill from the farm.

'Well, you should be,' he said breathlessly. 'Because that's not all. Darragh has just phoned Mam,' he said, mentioning her youngest older brother, who worked at a bank in Wexford. 'The manager wanted him to inform you, there's been a huge deposit in your account. He says you should come in to speak to their investment advisors—as it makes no sense to leave it there.'

'What?' She stared at him blankly, not sure she'd heard that right.

'Darragh says it's millions of euros. It has to be coming from him, for sure,' he added as his lips tilted in a mischievous smile. 'Unless you've been trapped in some other billionaire's love nest we don't know about.'

'Oh, shut up, Connor.' She stalked past him, the nausea building under her breastbone.

Why would Logan give her money? It made no sense.

She dragged her phone out of her back pocket, switched it on. News notifications popped up, the headlines hitting her like bullets.

Billionaire Recluse Goes Home to the US

The Colton Orphan Returns from Lapland Exile

ColtonCorp Heir Outed as Celebrated Wood Sculpture Artist LAC

But the pictures were so much worse. Logan at JFK airport, his head covered, as he was rushed into a waiting limo with bodyguards either side of him surrounded by the press. All those people, so many people, how could he survive it after so long alone?

She sucked in a breath, covered her trembling lips with her hand as she clicked on a photo taken through the car window and enlarged it.

Her breath clogged in her lungs. The pain in her heart clawed at her throat.

His eyes were all wrong, the fierce silvery blue now cold and empty and devoid of expression. Like a wounded wolf, defending what little territory it had left.

The vultures had besieged him. Forced him to face the trauma he had spent years protecting himself against.

Just as you tried to do, Cara, because of some foolish notion you could make him whole. When he was already whole.

What Logan did now, what he was forced to do, was none of her business any more. She wiped away the errant tear that leaked down her cheek, like too many others in the past three weeks, and clicked on the home screen to her banking app.

She gasped as the balance displayed.

She'd been close to a thousand euros overdrawn yesterday. Now her account was in credit by... Her brain short-circuited as she tried to register the amount. How many zeros was that now?

Connor whistled beside her. 'Cara, that's ten million euros.' He grasped the phone, began clicking. 'Comes from a numbered Swiss account,' he said. 'No name. But it has to be him, right? Where else could it have come from?'

She took the phone back, feeling numb, the smell of the elderflowers starting to grow in the nearby hedgerow doing nothing to stem the nausea in her gut.

What was the money for? Her silence? The sex?

Why would he think he owed her anything at all?

And why hadn't he contacted her to tell her about the money? Did he hate her that much now? He couldn't even speak to her?

She'd received no messages from him, even though she'd been stupid enough to check the post and her emails every day, just in case. Stupid enough to hope, against all the odds, that he might reach out to her, might need her.

If you change your mind, I will be waiting.

The phrase echoed in her head, only making her heart hurt more. But it fuelled her anger too. Why did she have to be the one to make the move? Why did it have to be her decision to make, and not his?

'It doesn't matter where it comes from,' she said, slowly, carefully. Her heart pulsed so hard in her chest she was surprised it didn't burst through her ribs. 'Because I'll be sending it back.'

She headed back across the fields she'd spent three solid weeks wandering in like a ghost, feeling guilty and compromised and heartbroken and alone, anesthetising herself against the vivid emotions Logan had awakened.

But they weren't anesthetised any more.

Connor jogged alongside her. 'Are you an eejit? That's a fortune. You can pay off all your debts and work on your pictures again. Why would you be giving that back now?'

She gathered pace, the purpose she'd lacked for the past three weeks, ever since he'd left her with that damn note, finally returning. He'd given her over ten million euros, a ridiculous amount, but hadn't even bothered to contact her, to tell her what it was for. Was it a bribe? A payment for services rendered? Because whatever way she looked at it, it was insulting. To her and to what they'd had, what they'd built together over those two glorious weeks in Lapland.

'Because I don't want his money,' she said, feeling scared and raw still, but also fierce and increasingly furious. 'I want him.'

Logan stared out at the rocky outcropping and the bay beyond from the roof terrace of the Colton Mansion in Rhode Island.

Built in the Colonial style in the nineteen hundreds, as a summer residence for his robber baron great-grandfather, the house had sixteen bedrooms, ten bathrooms, indoor and outdoor pools, tennis courts, a golf course—now covered in a sprinkling of snow— and a stone guest house on the edge of the ten-acre property where he had been living since his return to the US three days ago.

But he couldn't sleep in the stone guest house, any more than he had been able to sleep in his home in Finland...

Everything here was different from the steel and glass structure he had built in Lapland. The ornate furniture that had been covered in dust sheets for over twenty years, until a week ago. The dull, expensive pieces of art his father's mother had packed the house with long before he was born. The carefully manicured lawns and gardens that had been cared for by a ground staff of forty people for twenty years while no one lived here.

Even the light was different from the light in the Arctic Circle, not clean and bright but dull and grey. There were no Northern Lights here, no flashes of brilliant colour amid the startling starry night...

He had run here, believing he could somehow escape the pain...

But here as in Finland one crucial thing was exactly the same.

There was no Cara.

He turned away from the view as he heard Colton-Corp's managing director, Grant Andrews, step out of the terrace doors.

'Logan, how are you doing?' the older man asked, his breath frosting in the winter air.

'Good,' he lied smoothly. He did not want any more sympathy. Or suggestions on therapists that could help him 'adjust to his new role'.

The truth was, he hadn't made the decision to return to the US because the press had finally discovered his home. He had already made up his mind— less than a day after leaving Cara at the cabin—that he couldn't live in Lapland any longer, because everything had changed.

And she was the cause.

What had once been his sanctuary, his fortress, had become a prison. Because he couldn't hear her voice, couldn't see or touch her, and yet her presence suffused every space, every room, every single scent and sound.

At first, he'd resented her. And blamed her for his misery, the loneliness that had never been a problem before she had appeared in his life.

Why hadn't she taken what he had offered? If she loved him, why wasn't she prepared to do anything to be with him?

Memories of her and their time together had tortured him—so he'd taken the decision to leave Finland. To come back, to prove that it had always been a choice to live in isolation, that she had been wrong to suggest there was something about the way he lived that needed to be fixed.

The only problem was, returning here hadn't made the misery stop. Hadn't filled the huge hole she'd left in his life. If anything, it had made it worse.

He still wanted her. Too much. But it wasn't just a physical yearning. It was far worse than that. She had somehow hijacked his mind, and his soul too.

He thought about her constantly. So much so that

he'd had ten million euros deposited in her account in Ireland... And he wasn't even entirely sure why. Was it supposed to be a pay-off—because he'd had some vague notion of forcing her to sign an NDA, even though she hadn't spoken a word to the press about their time together?

Or was it even more pathetic than that. An attempt to force her hand, to get her to contact him, because he wanted her back, so much, but he had no idea how to reach out and ask her...beg her, even, to come back to him.

How could he have become so dependent on one person, in such a short space of time, after being alone—and happy—for so long?

Because you were never happy...you were hiding.

The damning truth whispered through his brain, making him tense as he followed Andrews back into the study and closed the terrace door. The study where he was supposed to be pretending to take an interest in a seminar on ColtonCorp's investment strategy for the next fiscal year—but which had begun to bore him in seconds.

The Colton Corporation had been managed well for twenty years by a board of trustees, and, whatever the press said, he had no intention of taking the helm. But, unfortunately, his work as a sculptor held no pleasure for him any more either.

His life was in flux. He had no purpose, and no interest in finding one any more.

All of which was Cara's fault too.

'I'm glad you're adapting,' Andrews said, although Logan could see wary concern in the man's eyes.

Grant Andrews had clearly been chosen by the board several years ago to oversee ColtonCorp's vast investment portfolio because he was not an imbecile, and he knew how much Logan hated the press intrusion now he was back in the US…

What the man didn't know was that everything Logan had once feared so much—the loss of freedom, the press attention, the constraints on his movements, the constant social interactions that would push all the memories from the night his parents had died back to the forefront of his consciousness again—didn't scare him nearly as much now as the thought of spending the rest of his life alone. Without her.

'I left a couple of messages on your cell this morning,' Andrews said. 'But you didn't respond to them.'

'What messages?' Logan growled. 'I do not use the phone.'

Being constantly available and connected to other people by that thing was something he doubted he would ever get used to.

'Messages about Miss Doyle,' the man said.

The mention of Cara's name detonated in his chest like a nuclear bomb.

'Cara has contacted you?'

His MD nodded. 'Her bank returned the funds we transferred two days ago apparently. Although no one bothered to inform me until this morning. And I've just had an email from her, personally, demanding to see you.'

'What?' he said, his voice cracking on the painful burst of hope.

But the shock of hearing her name—and discovering she had not accepted his money—was nothing compared to the thought she might be nearby, close enough to touch.

'Cara is in the US?' he asked.

Grant nodded again but looked supremely uncomfortable. 'Actually, she's at the gatehouse. I spotted her as I drove up here. According to the guard, she's threatening to sue ColtonCorp if we don't let her in to see you. You need to make a decision, because if the press get wind of it, we'll be besieged again and we've only just got them off our back.'

Logan barely registered the last of the man's words though, because he was already charging towards the door of the study. His heart hammered his throat as adrenaline surged through his body, for the first time in over three weeks, ever since he had left her, lying in his bed. And he'd made the decision not to wake her. Not to try and persuade her to stay with him, one last time.

The wrong decision, he realised with a stunning burst of clarity.

He raced down the stairs, the sound of his footsteps echoing around the empty house, and threw instructions over his shoulder. 'Tell them to drive her to the house, then you must leave,' he managed as the combination of anger and hurt, guilt and desperation, threatened to strangle him.

She had come to him. And he would not give her a choice to leave him a second time.

He could not. He needed her. Now more than ever.

Because he couldn't function alone. Not any more.

He was only half a man—had *always* been half a man—without her. He knew that now. And he wanted to be whole again.

Cara climbed out of the car, not waiting for the security guard to open the door.

Nerves assailed her as a tall man in a business suit appeared from the imposing entrance to the huge mansion at the end of the spit of land.

The house, with its ornate gables and elegant, austere façade, was intimidating.

But not as intimidating as the man as he headed towards her across the frozen lawn.

Logan.

But not Logan. Not as she remembered him. This man was clean-shaven, his once long wavy hair shorn close to his head. And he wore a suit, the jacket lifting in the chilly wind, and flattening against his big body.

Her heart pulsed hard, battering her ribs, as he came close enough for her to register his expression. Not blank. Not the way it had been in the press photos she'd scoured a dozen times while on the budget flight to Boston she'd caught early this morning in Dublin.

It had taken her two bus rides to get here from Boston airport. Her stomach rolled over as she debated the wisdom of coming all this way. Of being so determined to see him again. She tried to find the fury that had gripped her two days ago, when she'd made the decision to come. But it had died during the long journey. Until all that was left was sadness, and confusion and guilt... And the endless regret.

He stopped in front of her. His jaw clenched tight as his gaze roamed over her.

Was that heat, longing, she saw in the steely blue? Or accusation?

A shiver ran through her, although she had on her winter coat. And was dressed a lot more warmly than he was. How could he look so invulnerable, dressed only in his indoor clothes?

He nodded to the security guard behind her, dismissing him. As the man left, and she heard the vehicle drive away, she wrapped her arms around her body, the chills running through her now not from the cold, but his fierce perusal.

He took her arm. 'Come inside, before you freeze,' he said. Her breath shuddered out as the familiar yearning pressed at her chest from his touch, but she didn't stop him as he led her into the house.

The place was enormous, the vaulted ceilings, the antique furniture, the sombre lighting, the smell of old wood and lemon polish, so different from the clean, unfussy lines and open airy spaces of his home in Finland.

She couldn't picture him here, not at all. Couldn't imagine he could be happy here.

But she forced herself not to say anything. His happiness was no longer her concern.

He led her into a library off the main hallway. The

view across the sound through mullioned windows took in a pool, covered for the winter, and the rocky coastline, a private beach. She'd always know he was rich, but this was next level. And only intimidated her more.

'Cara?' he said, turning and propping his backside against the desk. He folded his arms over that broad chest, making her too aware of his body in the tailored suit. 'Why are you here?'

The direct question finally unlocked the blockage in her throat.

'The money. Ten million euros, Logan? What was it for?'

He sighed, then stared down at his shoes. Bright flags of colour hit his cheeks as he shrugged. 'I think,' he said at last, his gaze finally meeting hers again, 'it was an apology.'

She was taken aback, but only for a moment. 'An apology for *what*, Logan?' she cried, the anguish that she'd kept locked in her heart during the long journey making her voice crack. 'For letting me fall in love with you? For letting me ruin your life?' she asked, the tears stinging her eyes. The last of her anger crumbled, breaking open inside her… Because she'd never been angry with him. She'd only ever been angry with herself. Why hadn't she taken the risk? Gone back with him to his home? Taken a chance on love? Why had she needed guarantees? Why had she wanted him to change? They could have had a good life there, she could have pursued her photography, her passion and…

'If it hadn't been for me,' she said, 'you would still be in Lapland. Still be safe.'

'Stop.' He grasped her hand, yanked her into his body, then wrapped his arms around her. 'Stop, Cara. I was never safe there, I was simply hiding, because I was a coward. You were right.'

'That's not true, Logan.' She stared up at him, the fierce intensity in his eyes turning them to a pale, silvery blue. She could hear his heart beating as he dragged her against his chest. 'I was the coward,' she said as she burrowed into his warmth. 'I was the one who was too insecure to trust her own feelings. I'm the one who should apologise.'

She banded her arms around him, pressed her face into the clean linen of his shirt. Wanting to hold him for ever and never let him go.

'Why should you apologise,' he said, his voice husky with emotion, 'when all you did was make me face the truth?' He grasped her cheeks, dragged her face up. His gaze was so expressive, so full of feeling now, she felt her heartbeat gallop into her throat. 'I was terrified of living,' he added. 'Terrified of confronting the past. Terrified even of being touched. I shunned people because it was so much easier to be alone. So much simpler to avoid the emotion of others, when I could barely deal with my own.'

'Because you suffered a terrible trauma as a young child, Logan,' she interrupted him, unable to bear the self-disgust in his voice. 'You learned to cope the only way you could. There's nothing wrong with that,' she said, wanting him to see who she saw when she looked at him, not that broken child, but a strong, resilient man. 'It was wrong of me to make you think that wasn't enough.'

'Yes, I learned to cope… But at what cost?' He let out a harsh laugh, the sound painful, the shudder of emotion making her hold him tighter, trying to absorb the pain of that traumatised boy that swirled in his eyes. 'My solitude became my sanctuary for so long that, when my grandfather died, I did not want to return here…'

He looked around, the emotion in his gaze raw enough to make her shudder, but when his gaze met hers again, the turmoil had passed to leave only the bone-deep yearning that yanked at her own heart. 'But this is just a place, like any other.' He cupped her jaw. 'My grandfather helped me to cope, the solitude taught me how to heal. But *you*, Cara, you taught me how to live. I know this because, without you there, the silence became oppressive. The tasks I had once found so fulfilling no longer mattered to me. My bed was empty. But my life was emptier still. I even missed your inane chatter.'

'Inane chatter?' she asked, trying to sound offended, but unable to contain the joy spreading through her like wildfire—at the longing in his eyes he was making no effort to hide.

'Mostly…' His wry chuckle folded around her chest like a hug. 'I didn't come back here because the press found me. I came back to escape from the loneliness I found there without you.'

Her heart bounced in her throat, the bubble of hope becoming a boulder. 'Did you?' she murmured.

'The money was an apology,' he said again. 'An apology for leaving you that morning without a word. An apology for demanding you live in isolation with me. For pretending that all I ever wanted from you was sex. When there is so much more I need. An apology for leaving you to face those bastards alone. But the money was also a pathetic attempt to force your hand, to get you to acknowledge me...' He huffed. 'Because I was too much of a coward to contact you myself and beg you to come back to me.'

She reached up, and clasped his cheeks, pulling his lips to hers, then whispered against his mouth. 'Ask me again, Logan.'

'Stay with me, Cara?' he said, the questioning tone crucifying her.

'Yes.' She threw her arms around his neck, and as he grunted and grabbed hold of her instinctively she whispered in his ear. 'Now just see if you can get shot of me a second time.'

The snow fell in fat, heavy flakes outside, with night falling over the Colton Estate. But several hours later, as Logan lay on the library rug, drawing circles over Cara's naked hip as the firelight flickered over her pale skin, and she slept like the dead, he realised he had found a real sanctuary at last.

Because his sanctuary, his home, his safe place,

wasn't in Rhode Island or Lapland, or anywhere in between, it would always be where this strong, smart, fierce, beautiful woman was—so close to his heart.

EPILOGUE

Eighteen months later

CARA STARED AT the two clear blue lines on the pregnancy testing stick. Then pressed shaking fingers to her lips. She bit into her knuckles, hard enough to leave a mark—the tumultuous combination of shock and joy and panic impossible to contain.

She was pregnant, with Logan's baby. And she had absolutely no idea how he would respond to the news.

The last year had been nothing short of...*idyllic*. That wasn't to say they hadn't argued at times.

They were both strong-willed, determined individuals, who had never had to compromise their desires before now. So they'd clashed more than once in the last eighteen months as they adapted their lives—so that they could live together.

First there had been the argument about whether Logan needed some therapy. She'd won that one outright when he had struggled with the nightmares that had come back with a vengeance, after the press ordeal that had continued to rage on and off while they were living in Rhode Island.

Then they'd clashed about whether they should return to Finland. With him insisting he had no need to return to Lapland, even though she knew the opposite was true. He had wanted to prove he could live with people, for her. But she could see the toll it took on him, not just the nightmares, but also the stress of living in a world where he was constantly 'available'. She'd eventually won that one too—by simply telling him the truth, that she wanted to return to the house in Finland as well. That her career required it, and so did his, because she knew he struggled to focus outside his workshop. And she loved the quietness, the solitude—and he was more than enough for her.

But even their disagreements had felt constructive—because they were the sort of wild, passionate arguments that always led to lots of great make-up sex.

But this news was different.

She glanced out at the landscape beyond the glass, the huge lake that surrounded their home on the edge of the forest. The cabin where they had used the sauna to warm up for their ice swimming now doubled as a storeroom for the kayak Logan had purchased recently for the camp-out they'd been planning ever since the snow had finally melted a few weeks ago.

In May, this far north, they now had over eighteen hours of daylight.

She pressed her shaky palm to her still flat stomach, realising that this baby would be born in February—while they were back in the grips of winter.

Their baby.

She let out a careful breath.

How did she broach the subject of a child with him, when they hadn't planned this? Hadn't even spoken of it... And he'd endured so much change already. For her.

She must have slipped up with the timing when she'd chosen to change her contraception. And all the spectacular make-up sex had done the rest.

The spurt of joy began to diminish. Considerably. As the panic and anxiety charged to the fore.

She didn't want to put any more pressure on him. He had worked so hard to exorcise the demons from his childhood, they both had. But how would he adapt to this new responsibility? What if he disappeared back into the shell he'd once used to protect himself from feeling too much...? And how did she deal with the fact that she didn't think she could give him a choice?

When her period hadn't arrived, the possibility of a pregnancy had slowly begun to dawn on her. And it hadn't taken her long to realise she wanted this baby.

She jumped when there was a knock on the door.

'Cara, what are you doing in there? If you wish to arrive at the campsite before nightfall, we must go soon. It is not safe to travel through the gorge at night,' he said in that typically protective tone.

'Okay, Logan. I'm coming.'

She dumped the stick in the waste bin. And washed her hands, still stalling.

When she finally got up the guts to leave the bathroom, he was gone. Probably finishing loading up their supplies for the camp-out they had arranged to observe the bears as they emerged from hibernation and began mating.

She finished packing her own backpack, then left the house. She trudged round the edge of the lake, but her steps slowed as she spotted him coming towards her. In a plaid shirt, worn jeans and work boots, the long hair she adored touching his shoulders, he looked more like a rugged mountain man than the heir to a billion-dollar fortune.

Her rugged mountain man.

You have to tell him you're pregnant now it's official.

He grinned, the spontaneous smile whenever he saw her just one of the many changes from the guarded, wounded man she had first met. Changes she had come to adore.

Logan was so much more open now. He still hated to talk about his feelings... But at least he was no longer afraid to admit he had them.

She couldn't bear to risk losing that man, even a little bit.

He pressed his callused palm to her cheek, the unguarded affection in his eyes making her heart stutter.

'At last you are here,' he said, the amused frown making her own heart ache. 'The bears will not wait for ever, you know.'

She swallowed. She had to tell him now, before she lost her nerve. Whatever the consequences they would work through them, together, because that was their superpower now.

So as he leaned in to kiss her, she pressed her palms to his chest—the arousal something she didn't want to encourage… For once.

'Cara, what is it?' Logan asked as Cara pushed him away. And avoided his kiss. 'Is something wrong?' he asked, aware of the panic in his own voice. The panic he had kept ruthlessly at bay for close to a week.

Something wasn't right. Cara had been quieter than usual for days now. The inane chatter he loved drifting into silence too many times to count. Plus she'd made a trip to Saariselkä yesterday, and had insisted on travelling there without him.

She'd told him it was a routine meeting with the rep from the stock photography site she now supplied. But he suspected it had been more than that, because she had clung to him this morning, after they made love, so tightly, then disappeared into the bathroom.

She had been so excited about the camp-out they had planned to observe the bears. Until a week ago. But what had changed?

She blinked, and he could see guilt shadow her eyes.

'Whatever it is, you need to tell me,' he demanded now. She was scaring him.

The last year and a half, with her, had been the best eighteen months of his life. Bar none. Everything about her still fascinated and excited him. And there was nothing he would not do for her… Even agreeing to see that nosy shrink, who had forced him to talk about his feelings for hours on end.

He wasn't hiding any more, he was living. He had no fear of people now. Although he had no specific need to spend too much time with any of them. Except her.

Was that it? Had she begun to feel smothered? Her life curtailed by his need for solitude? This was precisely why he had not wanted to return to Finland full time, even though he had missed the quiet and serenity here. He hadn't wanted to risk the chance that she would feel suffocated.

But she had seemed to enjoy it here too. They had both become immersed in their work and building their life together. He hadn't seen the signs.

He cursed silently as she continued to look at him. Of course, he hadn't seen the damn signs. Because he was still learning. How to negotiate rather than demand. How to temper his desires, and adjust his own needs so he didn't risk overwhelming her.

But she had seemed as enthusiastic about their life here. How could he have been so wrong?

He watched her swallow, unable to stop himself from cupping both her cheeks now, from touching her.

She grasped his hands and pulled them away from her face. 'It's okay, Logan… It's… I don't want to scare you. But I have news that you might not… Well, you might not like.'

'Tell me,' he said, unable to keep the edge from his voice.

If she was going to tell him she was leaving him,

he might have to kidnap her, he decided—completely irrationally—as the panic began to consume him.

'I'm pregnant,' she said.

'You're…*what*?' he rasped, not sure he had heard her correctly, even as the pressure in his chest released in a rush, to be replaced by the instinctive spurt of joy and excitement.

Had she just told him she was having his child?

His gaze dropped to her belly. Her very flat belly. As his hands lowered to bracket her hips the thought of seeing her become heavy with his baby, of watching it grow inside her, made the spurt of joy turn into something so strong and fluid and powerful he couldn't speak. He could only feel.

'I… I'm going to have your baby, Logan. I know it's not something we've talked about. If it's too much… If you don't want to become a father you have to tell me, and I hope we can figure it out together… But I want this baby, because this baby is part of us. And I love us so much…'

She was talking, babbling really. The chatter he loved was back. But it wasn't inane any more. It was filled with love and possibilities… So many glorious possibilities.

'Please, Logan, say something.'

He raised his head at last. And looked into her eyes, the smile spreading across his face like the sun that had risen early that morning and bathed the landscape in glorious light.

He couldn't talk though, because his heart was

jammed in his throat. So he gave her an answer the only way he knew how.

He cradled her face, drew her into his embrace and captured her mouth. The kiss was hungry, famished, but as he fed on her sobs and sighs, felt the tension and guilt melt from her body, it also became full to bursting with hope and excitement and joy.

When they were finally forced to come up for air, he rested his forehead against hers. And wrapped his arms around her hips, until she could feel exactly how much he wanted her. Always. And for ever.

She had given him so much already…he had never believed there could be more. Who knew?

'I'll take that as a yes,' she said, and the laughter in her voice echoed in his heart.

* * * * *

If you were intoxicated by the drama of
Undoing His Innocent Enemy,
*then you're sure to adore these other stories
by Heidi Rice!*

A Baby to Tame the Wolfe
Unwrapping His New York Innocent
Revealing Her Best Kept Secret
Stolen for His Desert Throne
Redeemed by My Forbidden Housekeeper

Available now!

#4169 THE BABY HIS SECRETARY CARRIES
Bound by a Surrogate Baby
by Dani Collins

Faced with a hostile takeover, tycoon Gio must strengthen his claim on the Casella family company with a fake engagement. He'll never commit to a real one again. Despite his forbidden attraction, his dedicated PA, Molly, is ideal to play his adoring fiancée. The only problem? Molly's pregnant!

#4170 THE ITALIAN'S PREGNANT ENEMY
A Diamond in the Rough
by Maisey Yates

Billionaire Dario's electric night with his mentor's daughter Lyssia was already out-of-bounds. But six weeks later, she drops the bombshell that she's pregnant! Growing up on the streets of Rome, Dario fought for his safety, and he is determined to make his child equally safe. There is just one solution—marrying his enemy!

#4171 WEDDING NIGHT IN THE KING'S BED
by Caitlin Crews

Innocent Helene is unprepared for the wildfire that awakens at the sight of her convenient husband, King Gianluca San Felice. And she is undone by the craving that consumes them on their wedding night. But outside the royal bedchamber, Gianluca remains ice-cold—dare Helene believe their chemistry is enough to bring this powerful ruler to his knees?

#4172 THE BUMP IN THEIR FORBIDDEN REUNION
The Fast Track Billionaires' Club
by Amanda Cinelli

Former race car driver Grayson crashes Izzy's fertility appointment to reveal his late best friend's deceit before it's too late. He always desired Izzy, but their reunion unlocks something primal in Grayson. Knowing she feels it too compels the cynical billionaire to make a scandalous offer: *he'll* give her the family she wants!

HPCNMRA1223

#4173 HIS LAST-MINUTE DESERT QUEEN
by Annie West
Determined to save her cousin from an unwanted marriage, Miranda daringly kidnaps the groom-to-be, Sheikh Zamir. She didn't expect him to turn the tables and demand she become his queen instead—and now, he has all the power...

#4174 A VOW TO REDEEM THE GREEK
by Jackie Ashenden
The dying wish of Elena's adoptive father is to be reunited with his estranged son, Atticus. Whatever it takes, she must track down the reclusive billionaire. When she finally finds him, she's completely unprepared for the wildfire raging between them. Or for his father's unexpected demand that they marry!

#4175 AN INNOCENT'S DEAL WITH THE DEVIL
Billion-Dollar Fairy Tales
by Tara Pammi
When Yana Reddy's former stepbrother walks back into her life, his outrageous offer has her playing with fire! Nasir Hadeed will clear all her debts *if* she helps look after his daughter for three months. It's a dangerous deal—she's been burned by him before, and he remains the innocent's greatest temptation...

#4176 PLAYING THE SICILIAN'S GAME OF REVENGE
by Lorraine Hall
When Saverina Parisi discovers her engagement is part of fiancé Teo LaRosa's ruthless vendetta against her family's empire, her hurt is matched only by her need to destroy the same enemy. She'll play along and take pleasure in testing his patience. But Saverina doesn't expect their burning connection to evolve into so much more...

Get 3 FREE REWARDS!

We'll send you 2 FREE Books __plus__ a FREE Mystery Gift.

FREE Value Over **$20**

Both the **Harlequin® Desire** and **Harlequin Presents®** series feature compelling novels filled with passion, sensuality and intriguing scandals.